THE WEEKEND GIRL

and other stories by

Marie Sheppard Williams

The Weekend Girl and Other Stories
©2004 by Marie Sheppard Williams

Cover art by Holly Schwartz

Published by:
Folio Bookworks
3241 Columbus Av. S.
Minneapolis, MN 55407-2030
(ph) 612-827-2552
(f) 612-827-4417
(email) info@folio-bookworks.com
(website) www.folio-bookworks.com

"The Italian Story" was first published in *The American Voice*.
"The Book of Saints & Martyrs" (in somewhat different form) and
"The Weekend Girl" first appeared in the *Alaska Quarterly Review*.
"Weeds" first appeared in *The Yale Review*.

Publisher's Cataloging-in-Publication Data
Williams, Marie Sheppard, 1931-
The weekend girl and other stories / by Marie Sheppard Williams.
    1st ed. — Minneapolis : Folio Bookworks, 2004.
    p. ; cm.

ISBN: 0-9744986-0-2 (pbk)
Library of Congress Control Number: 2003113969

1. Women—Fiction. 2. Interpersonal relations—Fiction.
3. Short stories. I. Title.

PS3569.H477 A15 2004
813/.5408--dc22   0311

Printed in the U.S.A.

Praise for...
The Worldwide Church of the Handicapped
by Marie Sheppard Williams (Coffee House Press, 1996)

"... irreverent ... vibrant ... sensitive without ever approaching sanctimony..."

— *Publisher's Weekly,* starred review

"It's a wonderful book! ... I heard the voice of Sherwood Anderson often in *Church* ... a stubborn narrator burrowing in to understand the true life inside the story.... There's a little Walt Whitman in there too, the tenderness without foolish sentiment toward ordinary people."

— Bill Holm, Minnesota author of *Boxelder Bug Variations* and *The Heart Can Be Filled Anywhere on Earth*

"*Worldwide Church* is an absolute joy. I have been reading it all day ... and made a fool of myself at Starbucks because I was laughing so hard that tears ran down my face, and then I started to cry...."

— Anne Lamott, author of *Traveling Mercies* and *Bird by Bird*

"Marie Sheppard Williams' *The Worldwide Church of the Handicapped* is the product of a moral genius. It is one of the most important books of our time. And makes marvelous reading. The author is unmistakably one of those people whose love of kindness is no-holds-barred. . . . Don't be deceived by the fact that you are reading enchanting memoir: you're reading the thoughts of someone who hates cruelty."
– Carol Bly, author of
Changing the Bully Who Rules the World
and winner of the Minnesota Book Award

"Leading the reader past PC mental blocks is, for [Williams], like leading the blind past death: 'It is an act of pure service, economical, absolutely appropriate, not too much given, not too little.' . . . and [Williams] . . . is one of the best guides one could want."   – *Skyway News,* Josie Rawson

"At its best, Williams' style is akin to that of author/monologist Spaulding Gray. Both are superb storytellers who bring us into their worlds while they regale us with hilarious tales of bizarre situations and loopy acquaintances."
– *Columbus [Ohio] Dispatch,* Heidi Johnson-Wright, nationally recognized advocate for people with disabilities.

". . . You don't forget these stories. . . ."
– *St. Paul Pioneer Press,* Pj Doyle

"Her prose—steadfastly honest and spiked with irony—is alarming at times and inspiring throughout."
– *Minneapolis/St. Paul Magazine,* Becky Waller

"I'm cheering for this one at the World Olympics of Books."
— *Minnesota Women's Press,* Glenda Martin

"This is a wonderful book and should be read not only by rehab professionals, but also people who might like to become professional human beings."
— *Minneapolis Star-Tribune,* Dave Wood

"The stories are compelling, compassionate, caring, conflicted, and contemporary . . . Recommended for libraries and university collections at all levels."   — *Choice,* B. Harlow

"Beyond political correctness or incorrectness, [Williams] shows the way to an all-encompassing understanding of life's misfits—including ourselves."
— Sallie Bingham, author of *Matron of Honor*

"I have not, in a long time, read stories that affected me so much."
— Howard Zinn, author of *A People's History of the United States* and *Terrorism and War*

"This book should be required reading for every school of social work in the country. The author understands life at a level no psychology text can touch. The book is transforming. . . ."
— Merrilyn Belgum, MSW, ACSW, Professor (retired), University of Minnesota School of Social Work

["Williams'] characters are unique and unforgettable. This is a disarming, disturbing book."
— Maxine Kumin, author of *Women, Animals, and Vegetables*

"... satisfying ... a remarkable level of achievement...."
— *Georgia Review,* Erin McGraw

"... Highly recommended! I've read nothing else like it."
— *Notes from the Pond,* Liza at Orr Books in Minneapolis

"... I finished Williams' book feeling much the same as I do at the end of a Fellini film: confused, enlightened, hesitant, eager, depressed, delighted, and overwhelmed ..."
— *The Corresponder: a Fan Letter on Minnesota Writers,* Donna R. Casella

"... The stories are tough and complex ..."
— *Minnesota Monthly,* Laurie Hertzel

"... [Williams] has written a short story collection that is hard to describe and impossible to put down.... a perfect blend of honesty, humor, and poignancy...."
— *Disability Resources Monthly,* Sally Rosenthal

"... [These] are among the most extraordinary short stories I have ever read...."
—Wayne Gilbert, English teacher and writer

For Danny and Esta
and
for Megan, always

Acknowledgements

I would like to thank the editor of *The Alaska Quarterly Review*, Ronald Spatz, for originally publishing the title story and "The Book of Saints and Martyrs," the latter reprinted in somewhat altered form here. Thanks also to *The Yale Review* for "Weeds," which was my first published story. And last—never least—to Frederick Smock, former editor of *The American Voice*, which included the original publication of "The Italian Story." Fred has been a dear friend as well as an editor.

And affectionate gratitude to a lot of people who listened to, read, and critiqued these stories as they were being written, across a span of twenty years or so: Donna Jansen, Holly Schwartz (who also provided the cover art), Bob Williams, Megan Williams, Dan Ross, Lori Loughney, Cathy Camper, Elizabeth Petrangelo, Monica Woelfel, Lee Engfer, Carolyn Bell, Susan Hamerski, Carrie Pomeroy, Cia White, Wren Smith, Kristina McGrath, Barbara Jones.

Special thanks to Lori Loughney, who gave so generously of her time and expertise, and who suggested the device—"Nothing is stirring"—that absolutely *makes* "The Weekend Girl." (We are all of us—writers—thieves; but some of us admit it, and indeed, take pride in it.)

Thanks to Donna J., who helped with the proofreading, and who has been a staunch and unfailing friend and supporter—indeed, sometimes we call her "Sancho Panza"—all the years we have known each other.

Special thanks also to my publisher, Liz Tufte, at Folio Bookworks. She and I wandered into the unknown hand in hand on this project, and now I have not only a publisher, but also a new friend.

Author's Preface

Here are five stories. Or novellas. Or long stories. Or memoirs. Or even—bastard word—"fictoirs." I would go with "fictoirs" —the concept is pretty good—but it is such an ugly word.

I write what I write. I always have done. A rose, etc. I tried to write like everybody else early on, but without notable success. Most of the things I write about actually happened. Some didn't. Some of the things I remember as true, other people say never happened. So there you are.

I believe that fiction—some of it, anyway—tries to be the triumph of truth over facts. And with that in mind, these stories are fiction. I have told and written stories since I was six years old—I think in an attempt to make what I saw happening around me come out better. I have always looked for the right and perfect ending. Sometimes I find it and sometimes I don't. I use the techniques of fiction to present any facts that come to hand.

I have written about the same incident in two stories here; I don't know of any rule that says I must not do this. And if there were such a rule—hey, I'd do it anyway.

My very best to you as the reader. Without a reader there is no story. That sounds pretentious, but actually I believe it is just true.

— *Marie Sheppard Williams*

Contents

Weeds	1
That Summer	27
The Italian Story	71
The Book of Saints and Martyrs	119
The Weekend Girl	169

WEEDS

I

There are two very old ladies in my back yard. I am watching them from the upstairs window of my house. One of the ladies is my mother and the other is my Aunt Anna, who is also my godmother.

They are digging out weeds.

My mother, being a couple of years younger, only eighty-one, has the edge on Anna. She can stoop down, bending at the knees.

Anna is jealous of her sister. "Oh . . . ah . . ." she laments. Her voice comes to me clearly through the open window. Her voice is a rusty scream, there is a cry in it. "How I *envy* you, Elizabeth!" she wails. "You can still *stoop!* Oh, how I envy you!"

My mother murmurs an answer, which I do not catch: Anna probably does not hear her either, since Anna is rather deaf. So is my mother. Verbal communication between the two of them seems seldom really on target, seems always a little askew.

Anna is doing all right with the weeds, though. She has invented a system. She has commanded me to bring out into the yard a solid wooden kitchen chair; which I did carry out (protesting: no, no, you don't have to weed my yard; please don't weed my yard; please sit in the sun . . .). Anna clutches the back of the chair for support and then she bends over from the hips at a remarkable angle. She clings to the chair and reaches down to get at the weeds with an old sharp kitchen knife. She thrusts the knife in deep beside each dandelion root, each clump of crab grass, and then twists the knife to cut the root deep under the surface; and then catches the weed with the same hand that holds the knife and tosses the weed onto a growing pile. All the while she grasps the chair to keep herself from toppling over.

When she has cleared a little section as far as she can reach, she straightens up with a terrible groan and drags the chair a couple of feet to another spot and begins again.

A raucous shouted litany accompanies all this: and my mother's murmured answers are its responses.

"*Oh I hate weeds!*" screams my Aunt.

". . . hurt yourself . . ." my mother's soft voice.

Loud laughter, mocking: *I have always hated weeds! They are so stubborn!*

Torn thread of sound, plaintive: . . . *worth it?* . . . Anna catches this.

Loud: *Worth it? Worth it? Certainly it's worth it!*

I am here in the upstairs window of my house watching this and listening because I have fled the scene. The great chair idea broke me. I couldn't take it. My three cousins, Tildy and Lollie and Dolly, daughters of the two old ladies' older sister Catherine, dead thirty years, sit in lawn chairs and drink vodka collinses and watch.

Apparently they are made of tougher stuff than I am.

Afterwards, when I have persuaded my Aunt Anna and my mother to knock it off and to sit in lawn chairs in the warm

June sun of Minnesota, I give them cold glasses of lemonade; my Auntie says to me, "I *loved* that, Joan! I just *loved* that! If I lived in this house I would keep every single weed out of your back yard."

"I simply *hate weeds*," she says.

"I kind of like weeds . . ." I say.

Anna stares at me. "You must be crazy," she says.

"Joan is getting soft in the head," she says to my cousins. "In her old age." Then Aunt Anna grins. She looks at Tildy and Dolly and Lollie. "Joan has the nicest house of all of you girls now," she says nastily.

"Oh, now," says Tildy. "Heh-heh," she says. No way is she amused.

But she isn't as angry as she could be, either; Tildy likes me, really no matter what I do.

II

The women: Tildy and Lollie and their sister Dolly, daughters of Catherine; me, Joan, their cousin and Elizabeth's daughter; the Aunts—Anna, Elizabeth (my mother, aunt of my cousins), dead Catherine, and Irma, the baby, also dead. They (we) have separate identities, of course; but somehow it is more important that we all seem the same, branches of the same tree. I think of us in batches: the Cousins; the Aunts.

Tildy and Lollie and Dolly have other names of course, real Christian names, but they are always named together like that: Dolly and Lollie and Tildy. As children they chose those versions of the old-fashioned saints' names they were given: now we think of them only like that, Tildy and Dolly and Lollie.

III

I have an old family photograph in which my mother and Anna both appear. They are young girls: my mother looks about fourteen, and Anna could be sixteen. The young Elizabeth has a huge satin bow topping her delicately waving hair; she is small and slender and she smiles a half-smile sweetly and tentatively out from the picture. Anna is a head taller than her sister, and built much more strongly. Her long brown hair is in a thick braid wrapped around her head; her face looks out from under the lowering crown of hair, dark eyes stare beneath lowered lids. No smile here, nothing soft, but a sort of knowing look: heavy, sullen, passionate beauty. My path will be no path of roses, this sullen beauty says.

Much smaller sister Irma stands beside them in the picture, more delicate even than Elizabeth, younger than both of them; she has in the picture all the airs she kept when she was older, when I knew her: her head tilts to one side, her sly smile enchants. She is all feminine grace. One eye squints a little.

Baby sister Irma is dead now, under the ground five years. My mother sorted out Irma's clothes after she died; Anna wouldn't do it.

"You are so cold, Elizabeth," my Aunt Anna said to my mother at that time. "That you could do that. Pack up Irma's things."

"Someone had to do it," says my mother.

"You were always cold, Elizabeth," says Anna, weeping. "You were always hard, even when we were children. You had no heart. You were heartless."

My mother is terribly hurt.

"Do you think it is true?" she asks me. "No, of course not," I say. Yes, it is true, I think so. But Anna does exaggerate. It's not *that* true.

It is a year before peace is made between the two sisters. My cousin Tildy, whose mission in life it is to "keep the family together," works for months to bring about the peace. Me? I don't care enough. Besides, I think Anna is right, and I am obliged to say that my mother is right. I choose to ignore the whole thing.

IV

Grown old, my mother is still a small, slender, comparatively supple woman. She has never, she boasts, broken a bone in her life. I expect she never will. She falls, all right, and her flesh bruises, but her bones don't break.

Anna is a bigger woman, stout; her flesh hangs on her large frame. Her face, still remarkably unlined, has sunk into a sort of square. She wears dark-rimmed heavy glasses that do not help much; she can no longer see to read. The glasses are not flattering.

She wears a hearing aid that does not help much either. Like many people who do not hear well, she shouts.

She is diabetic. She does not care, she eats what she pleases. She lives in a small, crowded three-room house with her oldest son Cyril who has never married. Her legs are swollen from the diabetes, her ankles are ulcerated. She wears incongruous short white socks and old slippers. She can no longer tolerate shoes. One day when I was visiting her she shoved her foot out toward me:

"Look at that, Joan," she cried. "Look at that. Can you believe that I was vain of my feet and ankles when I was a girl?"

"I can believe it, Aunt Anna," I said. "I've seen pictures of you when you were young. You were beautiful."

"Catherine was the beauty, though," she said. "Do you remember your Aunt Catherine?"

"I remember her," I said.

"Catherine was much older than we were," she said. "Catherine was the beauty."

"I think you were more beautiful," I said. "Catherine was ordinary. You were—unusual looking."

Aunt Anna laughed—a short knowing squawk. Oh, I am unusual, she said. I was always unusual. Her bitterness was like a bracing, acrid tonic in the room.

I always liked you best, she said to me. You were always the one, with me.

I liked *you* best, I said.

You were like me, she said. You were the only one who was anything at all like me. My own children were not like me. Catherine's girls were not like me.

She sat silent for a second; she sighed.

Then: I wanted a daughter, she said. I always wanted a little daughter to dress up in beautiful clothes. I would have made her such beautiful clothes, my dear little girl . . . Her voice became a wail again.

I would have given her beautiful dolls, she cried. Oh, I wanted a little daughter so much. The wail has become habitual, conscious, comic. But the anguish is real.

She wiped tears from underneath the heavy, ugly frames of her glasses.

I never had a daughter, she said.

V

My Aunt Anna identifies with me. She thinks that we both have had tragic lives. I deny a parallel. I can't give her that. Good God, it would destroy me. I am for Christ's sake sorry enough for myself already.

I go to visit her with my mother maybe three times a year. We live in the same city, but on opposite ends of it. I am very busy, I work hard, I work as a social worker, it is a tough job, it takes all my energy. I help my mother a lot, take her shopping and what-have-you. This is where my duty lies. I don't see Aunt Anna very often.

Well, damn it, she upsets me. I don't need it. I can't do

anything for her; it makes me frantic with helplessness. What could I do for her? Shoot her?

When my daughter, sixteen years old, decided to go and live with her father, my divorced husband, in California, Aunt Anna was all mourning and sympathy.

You miss her, Joan, don't you? she said. You miss her *terribly*.

No, I said: Would I miss a toothache? That child made my life utter hell for a year before she left.

But your *daughter,* she said. I *know* you miss her.

I do not miss her, I said firmly. I caught my cousin Cyril's eye across the room; he and I often have extraordinary moments of hilarious contact. I have never known Cyril well at all in the way one usually knows people; he doesn't talk much; never did; but I *know* him, do you understand? We are in agreement about his mother. We think she is absolutely an old horror and crock; we are both crazy about her; our shared view of her is a total warm tie between us. We look whole conversations at each other.

— What can you do?

Shrug. Lifted eyebrow. Silent laughter.

— Nothing. There is nothing to do.

— Humor her?

— Punch her in the nose.

— Love her? Love a porcupine.

— Jesus Christ, is there any answer?

Grin.

— God, isn't she funny? Isn't she great? Isn't she awful? What can you do?

Joan, you have had a tragic life, my Aunt Anna persists. Just like mine. You lost everything you loved. You lost your first little son. You loved your husband and you lost him. And now you have lost your daughter, your darling little daughter . . .

Lies! my heart screams.

I feel really pissed, really angry. *No,* I say, loud; this I want her to hear for sure: I *have not had a tragic life, Aunt Anna. I have had a good life, an interesting life. My marriage was very good for a long time. When it wasn't good any more, I ended it. I did a good job bringing up my daughter, and when she was ready to go, I let her go. I feel good about it. I have a good life.*

No, no, she says, nods, grimaces, twists her hands in an agony of sympathy I do not want. I know, she says, that you have had a sad life.

Jesus god. I don't want this. I don't need this. I hustle my mother into her coat. I say goodbye to Aunt Anna, kiss that soft old eager avid cheek. I go. I have a feeling of abandoning my cousin Cyril to a desolation beyond telling.

My daughter Margaret, when she comes to visit, won't go with me to see Aunt Anna. It's too sad, she says. It's too terrible. It makes me feel like I am going to die some day.

VI

The earliest memory I have of my Aunt Anna is a memory of the wake held for her son Paul, who drowned when he was six. He fell under the ice of the Mississippi River in March and his body was not found until seven weeks later, late in April. I was just three years old. I did not understand anything of what was happening.

The casket was open; Anna wished it so, they say. I saw that my cousin had brown stockings on; his legs looked like sausages to me. They were swollen from being in the river so long, I later knew. "Mama," I said, "why are Paulie's legs so fat?"

"Shh," my mother said. "Aunt Anna will hear you. You'll make Aunt Anna feel bad."

Aunt Anna did hear, and apparently did feel bad; because she cried out and slipped from her chair onto the floor and sobbed, horrible, tearing, screaming sobs. Her husband, my favorite Uncle Luke, bent over her to try to lift her up; she fought his hands away.

"Please try, Anna," I heard my uncle say. "Please try to stand up."

He hovered over her helplessly, his hands making futile, clumsy gestures in the air above her, not quite daring to touch her.

"What is wrong with Aunt Anna?" I asked. My mother said, "Aunt Anna fainted."

What was "fainted"? What was "dead"? Why didn't Paul get up, if all this fuss was about him lying there in that pretty bed?

When my own first child died, there was no wake. No one was allowed to see the body except my husband and one of his friends. My Aunt Anna complained to me about this." I would have *loved* to see your baby, Joan," she said. "I would have *loved* to see him!"

"I did not want it," I said.

VII

The family like to say: Anna was never the same after what happened to Paul. They told stories about it for years.

All that seven weeks they were looking for him, my mother said, your Aunt Anna stood by her front door in the afternoons when the children were coming home from school. Every day she would stare off into the distance: I can see him coming Elizabeth she would say to me. I can see him just there—pointing down the street—he'll be here soon. Every day she would go to the river and call his name: *Paul! Pan-u-ul!* We were afraid to leave her alone (my mother said)—one of us always tried to be with her. She told me afterwards that that was the only way she could stand it, to pretend that Paulie was alive. She told me (said my mother) that it was the only way she could stay sane at all.

(But how sane was she? I'll never tell. We do protect our own in this family. She was pretty strange, I'll tell you that much; and that wail came into her voice then, they say, and never left it: that wild, deliberate, exaggerated, high-pitched, crying speech, with the odd thread of laughter, of terrible self-mockery, of laughing, longing, covetous pity in it.)

VIII

"Do you think we are an odd family?" asked my cousin Lollie one day when we four cousins, Lollie and her sisters, Tildy and Dolly, and I, were sitting at a ritual luncheon at Dolly's house in Richfield. Dolly is the oldest of us all, she must be nearly sixty, she is a widow, she lives alone. She has one daughter, Serene, married now, who turned out to be a lovely dark-haired dark-eyed girl, said to look like her grandmother, the beautiful Catherine. "*I* think we're a *very* odd family," Lollie said.

"You better believe it," I said. "I think we're *damned* odd."

"Why, what do you mean, *odd?*" said Tildy. "I don't think we're odd at all. I think we're very normal." Normal—that is one of Tildy's favorite words.

I laughed. "Well, I'm sorry," I said. "But I think we're odd."

"So do I," said Lollie. "*Very* odd."

"You always did like to say things that were just shocking, Lollie," said Tildy. "You always did, even when we were children."

"Oh well," Dolly intervened, giggling, "I don't suppose it matters . . ."

"What do you mean, it doesn't matter!" Tildy shrilled at Dolly. "You never think anything matters, you always give in! Of course it matters!"

I remember a story told of Dolly when she was a child, playing in children's games, and when the children would begin to sing out FIRST! SECOND! and so on, they say that Dolly, anticipating the worst, would say, Last . . .

I sat and ate my lunch and watched the sisters fight. I have to admit I enjoyed it.

We *are* odd. Take Tildy for example. She has decided that her husband Norman is psychotic. She has read up on it, and has decided this. She has gone from one psychiatrist to another, dragging protesting Norman behind her, until she has at last found a psychiatrist who (she says) agrees with her.

Norman's symptoms, as far as I can figure out, are that he keeps a diary, writes poetry, drinks some, and likes to flirt with other women. Poor old Norman, I have always liked him. Norman will not "cooperate in the therapy," so the psychiatrist says the situation is hopeless.

"What is your opinion, Joan?" said Tildy, once. "I mean, you're a social worker, you ought to have an opinion."

"I have an opinion all right," I said. "But I don't give my clinical opinions to relatives."

She kept at me, though. She wouldn't give it up. Come on, Joan, I really want to know, what is your opinion, please, tell me. Tell me.

Finally I gave in, exasperated to the point of meanness. "Well if you really want my opinion, Tildy, which I don't think you do," I said, "my opinion is that if there's anybody that's crazy in your house, it's you."

Her reply to that was terrific; I take my hat off to her. "What would you know?" she said. "You're not a psychiatrist."

Oh *god,* I said to myself; I was furious. With myself: suckered into that one, for god's sake. And furious with her: the truth hurts. I am not a psychiatrist.

I still like Tildy, though. And she still likes me. It's just amazing to me. Sometimes I think I push it on purpose, to see how far I can go. To see where love will end.

When I was divorced, and you still had to prove mental cruelty, no friend would testify for me. Tildy testified for me. Blood is thicker than water, my mother says. I would do a lot for Tildy.

IX

I am the chosen one; I am the front runner for this ghastly group. I swear that I do not know how this has happened; I was somehow elected when I did not even know that there was a contest. But it is true, it has happened, I am the one they are proud of, I am the one whose life they watch. If I do it, it may not be okay, they may not approve it, but it enters, I think, a sort of file called *precedents*. I like my position; it does not become tedious.

Examples? Well, marriage outside of the church, for example. First my own: horror, shock, outrage; then another: scarcely a ripple. Divorce: same thing. I was the first woman among us who went to college; then Tildy did. If I cut my hair a certain way, someone follows. Working at a job?—first me, then the others. Sometimes it becomes a little frightening: what am I doing, leading them astray from something that was solid and good? or conducting them bravely into a brave new world? But how can it be my fault, whatever the consequences are?—since I did not choose, since I was chosen.

All I know for sure is that when there is a party and I deign to come—a rare occurrence, I mean what do they expect, my god I can hardly stand them, I *have* to ration my time with them for purposes of self-preservation—then the party is a smash hit. It is an extraordinary feeling—to be this kind of success without in the least trying to be, without deserving it, without for heaven's sake lifting a finger except in my own interest.

I had a dream about them once. It was just at the time when I was first in the process of getting my divorce and going back to school to get a Master's degree. (A Master's! Wow, wow! Was that a knock-out? Were they proud of me? Oh, yes—they were. They simply marveled. Baby, you *can* go home again, I find, you *can* be honored in your own country if you happen to be a prophet; I can, anyway. And all comfort is there, at home; all love is there; if you can stand it.)

This was the dream: I was in a sort of temple. I was having a perfumed bath. I emerged from the bath, naked, dripping wet, clean, scented with strange exotic oils, onto a sort of stone terrace inside the temple. Suddenly I saw them: all my women relatives. They were coming toward me from all directions, down a stairway from a higher level of the temple, up from a garden, across the stone terrace: my mother, my grandmother, all the aunts, dead and alive, all the cousins, and *their* cousins, their daughters, my daughter, my sister who died, other figures more shadowy, whom I took to be ancestors from the long past.

They spoke no word, they only smiled at me, loved me, approved of me.

They had towels in their hands. They came to me with the towels and dried my body, toweled me dry, gently, delicately, smiled at me.

They did not speak at all, but the message was clear. You are ours. We expect something from you. We want you—to—

What? Why, nothing heavy, nothing hard. To be. To become. Myself. To grow beyond them: to be more.

I felt no weight: only honor.

But nothing hard? What could be harder?

In the dream I reached out my hands to them, one by one, and one by one they faded, disappeared:

Grandma? Reaching. Gone.

Dolly?
Mama?
Aunt Anna?
Irma?
Catherine?
Sister Dominic?
Tildy?
Lollie?
Margaret? (Margaret, stay . . . stay with me . . .)
Serene?
You? Who are you? A woman: who smiled, vanished.

I was alone: but not alone. A sort of benediction remained, a sort of ambience of approval. God. Can you believe it?

X

They say that Anna had a grand passion when she was a young girl. They say that her father, my grandfather, flatly forbade her to marry this man she loved; because, they say, in her father's judgment the man was a no-good. Even though he was a Catholic, incredibly, he was nevertheless perceived to be a no-good.

Can you imagine that the passionate, beautiful, strong, stubborn Anna would bend to her father's will? She did. She married instead of her true love a good Catholic man she did not love, my Uncle Luke. My Uncle Luke was a nice man, he was a barber, I remember him cutting my hair with the most delicate touch, no one ever again has cut my hair so satisfactorily, he loved being a barber, he changed and became a mechanic instead to make more money for Anna; but you see, Anna didn't like him, so nothing he did for her was any good, ever.

He bought her a house by the river, a nicer house than her sisters' houses. Paul drowned in the river, and then the house was bad, and the drowning was Luke's fault, he had bought the house by the river.

They sold the house by the river, they bought a smaller house, far from the river; Anna wanted money in the bank after that instead of the nicest house. I remember her after Paul's death, it was not so much that she turned against her other two sons as that she turned against love, against life.

She was terrible. She would talk, say terrible things to my mother, which I would hear.

Why did God take Paul? she said to my mother.

Why didn't God take one of the others instead? Cyril? Or Billy?

Do you think if I prayed hard enough, God would send Paul back and take Cyril?

Don't talk like that Anna, said my mother. It's a sin.

I don't care, said Anna.

They'll hear you, said my mother.

Anna refused after that death to take part in any of the ordinary rituals of love. They did not celebrate birthdays in that house after that, for example. They did not celebrate Christmas again, ever. No Easter baskets ever again for those two little boys who, through no fault of their own, remained alive, had not died.

She fed them, clothed them well, took care of them when they were sick, saw to it that they made their First Communions, their confirmations. She wouldn't love them.

Billy, married now and the father of three daughters, recently bought the grandest house that was ever owned by anyone in my mother's family. I went to see the new house.

"What do you think of the new house?" my mother said to me.

"Oh, well—comme çi, comme ça," I said.

"What does that mean?" said in my mother.

"It means I like mine better," I said.

XI

Houses are important in this family. Every one of us owns a house; nobody rents. Except my mother. When my father died, on his birthday, which was April Fool's Day, I was right in the middle of my Master's program. My mother thought I could help her take care of the house; I told her I couldn't. Could not.

I did not make her sell the house. I want you to understand this. I went out driving on the freeway with my brother one day just to yell this at him: screaming along the freeway in and out of traffic; I am a cautious driver ordinarily, but anger frees me. *Goddamn it,* I yelled at him, *I didn't make her sell the goddamn house! I didn't!*

I know you didn't, he said: Don't pay any attention to her.

Son of a bitch! I yelled, moving into another traffic lane. Back. Speeding.

Jesus, take it easy, said my brother. I know you didn't make her sell the house.

She says I forced her to! I shouted.

It's okay, it's okay, said my brother. (He's a really nice person, but he's like my father, he goes after that side, he's not entirely involved in this family; he joined his wife's family.) Listen, I believe you, he said, slow down, it's okay.

I hate her! I screamed. *I hate her!* Goddamn it I hate her.

Okay, you hate her, said my brother. Listen, that's okay. He started to laugh at me, there I was speeding along the freeway, yelling at him about our mother. Something very funny and cool about him hit me.

So I laughed too. Slowed down. Felt okay. Reasonably.

Thanks, love, I said. Thanks, darling.

My sister, he said. Wow, some crazy lady. Some crazy driver. Laughed again. We both laughed.

But I know how you feel, he said.

Maybe he does. Maybe he doesn't. Like I said, he's not exactly involved. He doesn't take responsibility.

I made my mother sell her house. What could I do? *Oh, forgive me, somebody. God?*

I don't know that any of the cousins would have let their mother, Catherine, move into a Senior Citizens' hi-rise. I was the first. This being first is some hell of an honor. This being me is something else. But I persevere. Can I let them down? Can I? Maybe it isn't okay; maybe it's just being a shit person?

My grandfather was an immigrant to this country from Germany. He was a shoemaker, and when he first came here he did something that was in one way dumb and in another way very smart. He bought two brick houses side by side on Third Street.

This was a dumb move because he chose the wrong part of the town for his brick houses; the area progressively deteriorated into a slum. He could never get a decent rent for his second brick house, and the people in the neighborhood were poor so he didn't make a lot of money in his shop either.

The smart thing was that he bought them at all. His children were the children of a poor shoemaker—but a poor shoemaker *who owned two brick houses.* There was solidity in that idea: everything else might go wrong, but they had a roof over their heads. And they were landlords. From the ninth-floor windows of my mother's hi-rise apartment I can still see those houses standing today when all their wooden neighbors have been razed, and I can feel a sort of comfort there.

Our grandfather owned two brick houses on Third Street: it comes up over and over again, in all the family tales. We have no fly-by-night heritage as in my father's family, whose members say: we were here before the Revolutionary War, we helped to build the great ship *Constitution,* we fought under John Paul Jones . . . we are brilliant, talented, crazy . . .

No, in the other family, we are solid, strong. We survive.

When my cousin Tildy and my brother testified at my divorce, they felt more or less bound by the truth, and there was nothing they could say against my husband's character, as a matter of fact they liked him, and as a matter of fact, so did I; but they hit on something else that really amazed me, and when I thought about it, it really *was* the reason: He made her live in an *apartment,* they said. He always made a good salary, *but he made her live in an apartment.*

When I got my divorce and went back to school I knew I was in for a tough time. Margaret, I said to my daughter, who was eight years old then, we have two choices. We can live on Welfare so that I can stay with you all the time; or I can go to school so that I can get a good job.

Go to school, said my daughter: I don't want to live on Welfare.

We'll be pretty poor for a long time, I told her. I'll be gone a lot. You'll be alone some of the time.

I won't be on Welfare, said Margaret.

You don't even know what Welfare is, I said. I don't care what it is, said Margaret: I don't like it.

God, I said, you sound like your grandmother.

When we really want to get insulting, my daughter and I, we accuse each other of being "like Grandma." You're just like Grandma, Margaret will say, and I'll react with a rush of fury every time.

Margaret, however, chose to ignore the shaft. Margaret is in all ways a stronger person than I am. She knew what she was after.

If you get a good job, will we be rich? she said.

Probably, I said. Compared to now, anyway.

When we get rich, will you buy me a house? said Margaret.

Marg, I said, if you hang in with me through graduate school, the first thing I'll do when I get a job is I'll buy you a house.

I did, too. I knew it was important. I put down the earnest money on a house just six days after I started my first job.

I was the first woman in our family to buy a house as a woman alone.

Houses are important.

XII

Aunt Anna is the only one of us whose ideas about houses are a little different from the ideas of the family. She keeps moving from one house to another; the rest of us buy a house and stay put. Also, each house she buys is a little smaller than the last; she makes money on every house sale; so she has smaller and smaller houses and more and more money. She gives the money to her sons. She says it is better that they should have it before she dies.

Aunt Anna's ideas about other things are different too.

We have a traditional event in this family that occurs sporadically; it is called a "get-together" and "the ladies" go to it.

The ladies are getting together at Tildy's house a week from Wednesday, my mother will say to me. I suppose you can't come.

You know I have to work, Mama, I say. She also knows that I take days off from work sometimes, for the hell of it, for my own pleasure.

That's what I thought, she says, miffed.

"The ladies": my mother; Irma when she was alive; Aunt Anna; Anna's daughter-in-law Myrna who is Billy's wife; my

WEEDS 19

three cousins; Dolly's married daughter Serene; me. Doris, my brother's wife, is invited every single time as a matter of courtesy, has been for the nineteen years of her marriage; she has never come. The ladies are—not hurt, exactly—*puzzled,* is more like it. I don't understand Doris, someone always says.

When are you going to have the ladies over? my mother used to say to me. So I've had them, maybe three times in all the years. That time with the weeds was the last time. It was always fun having them, it was always rather wonderful. And yet I resist "having the ladies." I just don't want to do it, even though I love doing it when it really comes down to it. There is something complicated in it that I fight, that I don't understand. There is something about loving it that means I am one of them, and I don't want to be, and I am.

When the ladies get together, something happens. Some hidden purpose is accomplished. It can be like an inquisition. It is all very sideways; but it is about as subtle as a thrown brick. They always mean well; Jesus I *know* they do but I can't stand it. I love it and I can't stand it. I end up furious every time; and loving them. The fury and the love are both uncomfortable.

One time, several years ago, right after my divorce, the get-together was for me. That is, the dark purpose was to do good for me; was to tell me what was expected of me. I didn't know ahead of time what they were up to. I was simply stunned when the beneficent brick hit me. I wonder to this day whether Aunt Anna knew what they were going to do: or whether her opposition too was staged, arranged. I swear to you: they are capable of that.

There I was, at Tildy's house, eating her excellent buffet lunch. Grace had been said, as it always is. Apostate and hypocrite, I mumbled it with them.

We were talking the other day, said my Aunt Irma. Me and Dolly were talking. Weren't we, Dolly?

Mm, yes, said Dolly: we were.

We were discussing, said Irma, whether a divorced Catholic who was married outside the church has the obligation to attend Mass.

Well, I suppose they do, said my mother. I mean, you are always a Catholic, no matter what. You can't stop being a Catholic.

Yes, said Dolly, and if you are married outside the church it isn't really a marriage anyway, and so it can't really be a divorce, can it? What do you think, Joan? she simpered.

I wanted to hit her. Sometimes I think I really hate Dolly.

Oh, well, I said. How would I know?

Well, *we* think they have an obligation, said Dolly: I do, and Aunt Irma and Aunt Elizabeth.

You too Mama.

I'd like some more casserole, I said. Tildy, this is a delicious casserole.

Oh thank you, said Tildy, really pleased. But what *do* you think in a case like that, Joan?

I don't have any thoughts on the subject, I said.

I think it's nobody's business but that person's, said Aunt Anna. Thanks, Auntie, I thought.

Oh, but we can't agree with that, said Irma. I mean, it can't all be left up to the person to decide.

Why not? demanded Aunt Anna. Why can't it be?

Well, because none of us are wise enough to know about things like that, said Irma, in her whiny, sly-little-girl voice; I have always had a sneaking belief that in a clever sort of way, my Aunt Irma was really somewhat retarded mentally; Dolly too. I mean (Irma said) the Church is wiser than any one of us.

(I could hear my father's voice: Joan, I've never given any of my children advice about anything, I know none of you would take advice anyway, but I just want to give you one suggestion, just a *suggestion,* out of my own experience: *don't marry a Catholic.* Well, Daddy, I didn't, and look what it got me—crucified at a goddamn *party,* for Christ's sake. *Oh, how I wanted to be a member of my father's family:* I tried to look like them; I tried to think like them; I tried to be creative and intelligent and crazy and free; but it was hopeless, home is where the heart breaks, aches, cries out for mercy; my mother's family is mine.)

Well, I don't think so, said my Aunt Anna doggedly. I think people have the right to choose for themselves.

Thank you, Aunt Anna, I said. Thank you for defending me.

There was a terrific uproar, everybody talking at once.

Oh, we didn't mean *you,* Joan!

We were just talking about a *case!* An abstract *case* . . .

Abstract. I'm surprised any one of them knows the *word,* for heaven's sake. They are about as capable of abstract thought as I am of turning lead to gold. (If you can't get them on any other front, attack their intelligence, that's my theory, you can never go wrong there . . .)

No, of course we didn't mean *you,* they chorused.

Why, whatever made you think we meant *you?*

We're so sorry if you thought we meant *you!*

Oh, god. You see what I'm up against? You see the pack that I am, by no will of my own, leading? You see the awful joke? You see?

Defenders and attackers together, they had accomplished their purpose: I felt horrible. I felt guilty. I felt cared about. I wished to Christ they would all drop dead.

When I was married, my Aunt Anna sent me a wedding present: a satin quilt for my marriage bed. No one else from the family sent me a wedding present. No one came to see me married except my brother, and like I said he's not really a member of the family. His wife doesn't come to the get-togethers.

XIII

I took a friend of mine to see Aunt Anna once, I had told my friend so much about Aunt Anna that she wanted to meet her. My mother was there too, of course she had to come, she is extremely jealous.

Some kind of discussion brought up the word: stubborn. Do you think I am stubborn? said my Aunt Anna. I sure do, I said. *I'm* not stubborn, said my mother; do you think I am stubborn, Anna? I think you're very stubborn, Elizabeth, said Anna. What about Joan? my Aunt Anna said to my friend: is Joan stubborn? Well yes I think she is rather stubborn: said my friend. Oh I don't think she is, said my mother. I do, I said: I think I am very stubborn. Aunt Anna laughed. Maybe we could have a Stubborn Club, she said. Only very stubborn people could belong to it. And she laughed and laughed. But my mother was mad for a week, and kept talking about it: I don't think I'm stubborn, she said. Maybe *you* are. Anna is. Not me.

XIV

One day not long ago I went to see Aunt Anna alone, my mother was not with me. I don't know, I just wanted to do that once, see Aunt Anna alone without my mother; I don't know why. I found her resting on the sofa with her feet up, her arms and legs terribly bruised. Cyril was home with her, he was waiting on her, bringing her tea for example. My goodness, I said, what happened to you? She wouldn't tell me, she looked for once shamefaced and embarrassed. Oh, nothing, it was nothing, she said. But what happened, I said.

She fell into the furnace grate, said my cousin Cyril. He gestured toward a metal grate in the floor, maybe a foot by eighteen inches. He laughed. I found her there when I came home from work yesterday, he said. Stuck up to her armpits in the hole, with the grate off.

Well for god's sake, I said, really it knocked me absolutely out. But how could such a thing have happened?

She was trying to clean it, Cyril said.

Clean it.

Well, I get so bored, said Anna. I get so tired of it all. I have to do *something*.

Joan, she said: You work with old people. Do they all want to live? Don't some of them want to die?

Yes, Aunt Anna, I said. Some of them want to die.

I want to die, she said.

Yes, I said. I believe you.

She smiled at me, such a smile, perfectly calm, perfectly sane, perfectly reasonable. I thought you'd believe me, she said. I saw Cyril's face for a second, turning away, twisting with tears held back.

Anna said: Don't cry for me when I die, Joan.

I won't cry for you, I said.

Do you think life is good Joan? she said.

No I guess I don't, I said: Not good, not that.

I don't think so either, she said. I haven't liked much of it.

I wonder if Elizabeth liked it, she said.

There was a silence. Then: I envy you Joan, she said.

Envy! I said. Me? I said. I was astonished. My god why? I said.

You've got a daughter, she said. I envied Elizabeth too, she said. I envied her you.

XV

I have in my mind very often lately a clear remembered image of the two old ladies digging weeds in my back yard that summer day; I can see them now, I guess I'll see them there forever, or as long as I can remember anything, the scene *sticks* so: the two of them, my Aunt Anna and my mother, Elizabeth, sisters of dead Catherine, both of them digging away at the weeds, my mother stooped down, my Aunt Anna jackknifed in an improbable bend, hanging onto her wooden chair. Tough, my god, strong; where do they get their strength? Listen, what will kill them? What in the world will kill them? Will they never die? Will I never die? Jesus I absolutely reject that thought.

    I have an idea about weeds: I think that I would like to plant a garden with nothing in it but weeds: a row of dandelions, a row of thistles, a row of quack grass: and water them, and pinch them back, and keep them in straight rows and mulch them and hoe them and talk to them. Well: I would *take care of them,* that's what the idea amounts to, be careful of them, value them. Listen, what would happen? If I did that? The thing is, if someone was careful of them, if they had value, would they still be weeds? What would they be?
    I would like to know.

THAT SUMMER

I

We were on a special train going from Minneapolis across Minnesota and North Dakota and part of Montana into Yellowstone Park: Sidney and Sarah and Beth and I. At least, I think the whole train was special, that is the way I remember it now, but maybe it was just a few cars on the train, that probably makes more sense. In any case, the car we were on was full of college kids, sophomores mostly, who had been hired in Minneapolis to work at Yellowstone Park for the summer.

It was a two-day trip. They—we—had taken apart the seats in the car and arranged them on the floor so as to have some minimal comfort during the one night we spent on the train.

(Is it okay to do this? I said to Sarah. Is it okay to just—like—take the seats apart? Won't somebody be mad?)

(It must be okay, said Sarah: they're all doing it . . .)

Most of us were away from home for the first time. We were seeing the country for the first time.

Across Dakota. The Black Hills.

The buttes.

And then the mountains.

I woke up in the first dawn of the first morning in the West —at maybe three a.m., maybe four, about that time, really early—and I looked out the window and saw the mountains. I remember waking, stiff and uncomfortable, sprawled on the floor, half on and half off a seat cushion, with the sound of the rails under me, ta-click, ta-click, and I saw all the other sprawled and draped sleeping bodies around me, my God where am I? and sitting up and looking out the window and there they were: the mountains.

Well, I had such a feeling: I can hardly tell you. It was like homecoming: I felt like I had been away and was now coming home. I, who had never been at home in the world at all, I was suddenly at home.

It didn't last, of course; in a couple of months I longed for the flat farmlands of Minnesota as earnestly as everybody else did; but on that first morning, somewhere crossing Montana, I was home.

I reached out my hand and touched Sarah, who was sleeping across half of my cushion. I shook her shoulder a little.

What, she said.

Cut it out.

Mumble, mumble.

Sal, I whispered in her ear. I know that you hate to be waked up. But this is an emergency.

I am doing this for your own good, Sal, I said.

Sarah and I both became social workers later in our lives; and you can see that in me at least the seed was there.

Get lost, she said. Muttered. Growled.

Well. We could go on and on here. But the point is, I felt that I had to wake her up and I finally did and she sat up and we sat there sharing a cushion and gazing out at the Rocky Mountains.

There was something magical about that morning waking. Maybe the thing that made it magical was that we didn't talk at all. We absolutely didn't utter a word. Well, and the thing is, we absolutely couldn't.

And we were each aware that the other could not speak, had no words: groped, gaped, and was still.

I guess it was probably kind of funny. If you had seen it from the outside. Even to us it was funny, in a kind of a way: years later, we remember, and we laugh.

I mean, honestly, we would (one of us and then the other) point out of the train window at the mountains, and our mouths would open and the word just wouldn't be there and we would gesticulate with both hands in the air in front of us where the word should have been and the word wouldn't be there. And we would close our hands around the word-space and our hands would come up empty that should have held this caught-fish word in them and there would be no word: I mean, what would the word have been?—marvelous? breathtaking? disturbing? alien? strange? No word covered it. None even touched it. The mountains were special: are still special, it seems to me, though I have never again in my life been back to see them. I have never wanted to go back.

Oh: you think I am carrying on like crazy about nothing much; but it wasn't nothing to us. Remember that we were young: no real events, really none, had happened to us yet. We had had no experience. We were—yes, we were—innocent. That old-fashioned word. Innocent. Honest to God: innocent.

So there we were, the two of us, with hands waving, groping, shaping astonishment.

Finally we stopped. Stopped with the hands. With the mouths. Relaxed into it and just stared out the window.

And then—together, absolutely together—we turned our dazzled eyes to one another and we looked at each other. Just the laziest, quietest, most surfeited look: and then a smile. A silly, satisfied grin. Together.

Oh.
Wow.
I give up.
Said the shared smile.

And that was how it happened that we saw the mountains together that first time, Sal and I. It has been a bond between us. Many years later we are still friends, and one of us can still say: do you remember that morning when, and the other can say, I remember . . . and once again we can sit and stare at each other and have no words.

II

I went to Yellowstone with three friends from the University of Minnesota: Sarah Olin—called Sal—and Beth Morelli and Sidney Garvey. Sidney was—is—a girl, but she was named Sidney by a couple of Alabama kids just before they abandoned her in a Birmingham bar and took off forever. Her name is Sidney Clare, they told somebody. The name suited her. Suits her. Sid would have been a splendid boy: as she has become, now that I think about it, a splendid woman.

Sarah and Beth and I worked that summer as chambermaids, and Sidney—who was there for her second summer and knew the ropes, in fact it was Sidney who convinced me and Sarah to come, she seemed to think it would be good for us—Sidney was a waitress. Waitresses made more money and had more status. Maids were the lowest of the low, and relief maids, which is what we were, were the lowest of the maids.

Sarah and Beth and I had to have been three of the most naive people alive that summer. Maybe still. And Sidney was the toughest and smartest cookie around Yellowstone. And any other place, any time.

I think Sidney was in a way ashamed of us. And thinking

about it, I can hardly blame her. She liked us, though—I've never really known why—and was gentle in her dealings with us; or at least she liked me and Sarah. Beth she hated.

She was so mad at us when we said we wanted Beth to come along that summer.

I can't stand that damn Morelli, she said.

Said many times.

Oh, Beth's all right, one of us would answer.

Sidney: No she's not.

What can you say? If you have no courage?

And the truth is, we liked Beth well enough to let her come along, but not well enough to defend her.

Sarah and Beth and I roomed together in a large corner room in Canyon Dormitory, and we learned more about each other that summer than we had ever really wanted to know. Sarah—for example—liked the windows open at night, and I liked them shut: who knew what was out there? Sarah and Beth were neat. I was a slob. Beth was into moving furniture —anybody's. I put a sign over my bed, which was unmade and piled high with clothes, souvenirs, etc.: *This is Joan's corner— Keep the hell out!* I don't know how we managed to remain friends through that summer. But we did. Sarah and I are still friends. Beth I haven't heard from for six or seven years. I've lost track of her; you know how that happens.

III

Beth had a crush on the Canyon Hotel wrangler that summer. She hung out around the paddock and the stables. We didn't see much of her except at night when she came in to sleep and at mealtimes.

Sarah and I stuck together: two odd ducks who had each

other. That can make for a happy adjustment to life, and I think in a way we were happy that summer. We were odd, but we were odd together.

Sidney avoided us all and ran with her own crowd. Like I said, she was ashamed of us. Dear old Sid; in a way she is still ashamed of us, but she is nevertheless loyal. To me and Sarah, that is.

Sidney still hates Beth.

Sidney, why do you hate Morelli so much? I said to her once, not long ago, maybe ten years ago, before Beth disappeared from my life. Sidney calls me now and then, she is teaching in a high school in Whittier, California, civics, I believe, something like that.

I mean, dislike, okay, I could see that, but you really just hate her, don't you? I said.

Yeah, well, I don't know, she said. I know what you mean, but I don't know why.

Over the phone, Sidney sounded baffled.

I simply don't know, Pooh Bear, she just royally pisses me off, that's all . . .

Said Sidney.

IV

Everyone was supposed to be twenty-one to work in the park that summer, but I can't think of anyone who really was. Everybody lied to get a job. Everybody was under age. Not just my crowd—but everyone.

And it was such a restless summer. We were always trying to think up something to do to relieve the terrible boredom and to justify being on our own. Charmion—one of the Mormon girls from Provo, Utah, seventeen years old with glasses and short curly red hair—Charmion developed a peculiar, aimless hatred for the dormitory maid, Mimi. And then, over time, it happened that because Charmion hated Mimi, we all did.

Motheaten old crock, Charmion would say.

Yeah, we would echo: old crock...

And: I saw Mimi this morning in the hall, Charmion would say: old bitch. I gave her the shit sign. You look like a can of worms, Mimi, I said.

Good, Charmion...

Once I said: Charmion, what has Mimi *done* to you?

Charmion rolled her eyes back into her head so that only the whites showed. (This was a trick she said she had practiced in the temple in Salt Lake to get out of services. I think it must have been very effective for the purpose, she did it so well, even when you knew it was fake it was frightening.) She pushed saliva to her lips and bubbled through it. She dropped to the floor like a sack.

Look what you've done! Charmion's older sister Jeanne gasped at me. Look what you've done!

(Jeanne's trick was hysterical paralysis—every time something happened to cross her will she became paralyzed on the whole right side of her body. We all got a very strange picture of Mormonism that summer.)

I'm sorry, I said. God. I take it back.

I gave Charmion, laid out on the floor, a little kick, harder than was perhaps strictly speaking necessary. Cut it out, Charmion, I said: I said I took it back.

Charmion continued to bubble.

Gosh, I think maybe she's really having a fit! Jeanne said, dropping to her knees beside her sister.

Gosh, I don't think so! I said. But I was a little scared anyway.

Sometimes she really does, Jeanne said. Charmion! Charmion! Jeanne slapped at Charmion's cheeks with the palms of her hands.

THAT SUMMER 33

Charmion opened her eyes, stopped bubbling.

Cut it out, Jeanne, she said.

I was really having a fit. She said. She sucked her saliva back into her mouth.

I thought you might be, said Jeanne, still kneeling, her long straight black hair hanging down over her sister's face.

Pfuh, said Charmion.

Get your hair out of my face, Jeanne, she said. Get away from me.

Jeanne stood up. See what you did? she said to me.

(What? Obviously nothing, right?)

I *said* I was sorry, I said. I *said* I take it back. I said.

Just so it doesn't happen again, said Charmion, in a faint, weak voice from the floor. Jeanne helped her to sit up.

I know who my friends are, Charmion said.

Charmion, I won't do it again, I said. God.

After that, I sort of hated Mimi too.

Everybody hated Mimi.

Mimi was horrible.

She had a face like a can of worms.

She didn't deserve to live.

It was so obvious. It was so clear.

V

There were all sorts of weird types at Canyon that summer. There was for example a woman named Lima Bee—I swear to God. Lima Bee was tough and jolly and held her own; nobody crossed Lima Bee.

There was a little guy named Henry who was almost a dwarf and who propositioned all the women by the end of the summer. As far as I know he had no luck except with one girl, Carolee, who was a pretty, faded little blonde. He called her Blondie. He told her he knew a movie producer who would give her a screen test and in August, just before we all left for home, she took off with him to go to Hollywood. The highway police stopped them a couple of days later in Coeur de Alene, in Idaho; we heard that later.

There was a middle-aged woman named Irene who was a waitress. Every time we saw Irene she was feeding the squirrels. This was funny, because there were nuts and stuff growing all over, there was plenty of food for all the little animals. Nobody needed to feed them. But Irene fed them; in fact, that was all she did besides be a waitress as far as we could tell was feed the squirrels.

And she bought expensive, special nuts for them—not peanuts or sunflower seeds or anything ordinary like that. Unsalted cashews. Hazel nuts. Like that. Pistachios.

We asked Sidney about her.

Who's the lady who feeds the squirrels, Sid?

That's Irene, said Sidney. Irene's crazy, kind of. She's been here for years. She comes back every summer.

Boy! that *is* crazy, said Charmion, giggling in a high-pitched squawk: to come here every summer, that *is* crazy . . . *ak . . . brak . . . gluck . . . vomit.*

That *is* crazy, echoed Charmion's sister Jeanne. *Ak, gluck.*

Irene's okay, said Sidney. But she's crazy.

Is she a good waitress? I asked.

Well, yes, sure, she's a pretty good waitress, said Sidney. Better than some.

Well, what I said, said Sidney: Irene is okay. She's not hurting anybody.

She's feeding the squirrels, said Jeanne.

Yeah, well, said Sidney: but that's not actually hurting anybody.

Still, said Jeanne.

THAT SUMMER 35

VI

We had to pretend that Canyon Hotel and Yellowstone Park were terrible places. Actually, they weren't; they were wonderful. It was a wonderful way to spend a summer.

We bitched about everything.

We said the food was terrible.

We said the work was too hard.

We said the management was taking terrible advantage of us.

Blah-blah. Blah-blah. Bitch-gripe. Piss. Moan. You know. Actually, the food was adequate. We didn't starve. We may have lost a little weight, but that was all to the good: we were always dieting anyway. We hardly worked at all: maybe three or four hours a day. Honesty was not the point here. The point was bitching.

We drank a lot of liquor, most of us for the first time in our lives. Mostly on Friday and Saturday nights in West Yellowstone. At, maybe, the Silver Dollar Bar, which had thousands of silver dollars embedded in its bar. Hundreds? Probably hundreds is more like it. Or dozens. Or the Stage Coach Bar maybe. The Wagon Wheel.

West was a tourist town, there were lots of bars. We went from one to another on a typical night, scrounging drinks from the tourists, who thought we were locals.

Nobody called it "West" except the people who worked in Yellowstone. The in-crowd. Us. *God: the in-crowd: us.* That felt so good. It feels good even now, remembering. The only other way I ever got to be an in-crowd member was by becoming a social worker and working my absolute ass off. And then I was only in with other social workers. That's like being in with lepers.

VII

Lord. We were so bored that summer. We were so unsure of ourselves. There's a good reason why the word sophomoric has come into being. I think I told you before that we were all sophomores: my crowd from Minneapolis, I mean, and actually most of the others too. Or even younger, some. We proclaimed loudly that we knew it all, and held secret the awful certainty that we knew nothing. Less than nothing. Zilch. Zip. Nada.

We were so scared.

Will I be all right in my life? That was the question that terrified. There was another question too: am I enough like the others?

One night some of us were just lying around on the beds and on the floor in our corner room, mine and Beth's and Sarah's. People migrated to our room, I suppose because it was the biggest room in the dorm. Me and Sarah and Charmion and Charmion's sister Jeanne were there, and Beth—the wrangler had gone off somewhere that evening and so Beth was with us for once—and Brenda Taft and Connie Ramirez, theatre majors from Pasedena—Brenda had met Tallulah Bankhead once, and Tallulah had said: according to Brenda, but who knew for sure?: Dahhhhling, do you fuck? and because of that Brenda was admired enormously, and Connie was admired because she stood next to Brenda. Both of them were pretty, and they had great dash.

Somebody had a pint bottle of brandy that night and we finished it off. We played catch for a while with the empty bottle.

Hey, Bren, *catch!*

Thunk.

Laughter.

Here, Beth!

Mimi and Mrs. Mason are in The Lobby, Connie Ramirez said suddenly. Connie was leaning out a window and she pulled her head back in to tell us this. Her long black hair caught and draped on the window frame. I just saw them go in. She said.

There was a grand entryway to Canyon Dormitory, God

knows why, called The Lobby. Maybe the dorm was something else once, like a hotel. There was a big carved center door flanked by two leaded glass windows. The door opened onto a big hall; and just off the hall was a sitting room where Mimi, the dormitory maid, and Mrs. Mason, the dorm matron, spent much of their time.

We all said they drank together in secret, but there was absolutely no evidence that this was true.

That Mimi, said Charmion. That crock of shit.

Yeah . . .

That ugly old can of worms . . .

I don't know how it happened, but all of a sudden a crazy idea was there.

Let's throw this old bottle through the window down there. . .

Oh, my gosh.

Silence. This was too much, nobody had the guts for this, not even loudmouth Charmion.

Then: I'll do it, said Beth.

What?

I'll do it.

You?

Beth laughed. She had a light, breathy, mocking laugh, like an echo from a covered well.

Why not me? she said.

So: indeed: why not?

We planned it all in just a few minutes, right down to Beth's escape, and it worked out fine and nobody got caught. The bottle shattered the big center pane of leaded glass in the panel to the left of the door and whizzed into The Lobby and missed Mimi's head—we heard later—by half an inch.

And a couple of minutes afterwards, when they came to look for whoever had done it, we were all asleep in our beds.

* * *

The next day, meeting at odd moments in corners in the hotel, we talked about it.

She could have been killed.

Beth could have killed her.

Yeah.

It was that close.

Oh, yeah, my gosh . . .

That's going too far.

No it isn't. She deserved it. (That was Charmion; I guess you figured that out.)

Uh-uh. That's going too far . . .

You would have thought that that escapade would have brought Beth some status, but it didn't. People spoke of the incident with awe, and laughed over it for the rest of the summer, but they didn't like Beth any more than they had before, which wasn't much. That was okay; she didn't like them much either. She spent her time hanging around the horses. And the wrangler.

It was like Beth didn't worry at all about whether she was like the rest of us. In a way I admired her for that. Secretly, of course. I never admitted any such thing publicly.

VIII

Charmion wore a boy's high school ring around her neck on a chain. She and this boy had decided to go steady just before she came to Yellowstone. In fact, it was because she was coming to Yellowstone that he gave her the ring. So that she wouldn't forget him over the summer.

We pledged our trust with this ring, said Charmion. And with my ring too, I gave him my ring too.

What's his name, Charmion? Sarah said lazily. Sarah (brown-haired, brown-eyed, slim, sort of luminous looking, with a sad and secret air about her, I always thought) Sarah sat cross-legged on the bed and stared out her window at the mountains that rose into the distance.

Claude, said Charmion.

Claude, I said. I poked Sarah and laughed: *Claude!*

Sarah turned then.

What, she said.

Charmion's boyfriend is named *Claude:* I said, and giggled.

Sarah laughed.

Hey: *Claude!* she said. Oh, my.

It's not such a funny name, said Charmion.

It is too, Sarah said. It's a hick name.

Easy tears came to Charmion's eyes and rolled down her cheeks.

Oh, come on, Charmion, I said. You're such a kid. Sarah didn't mean it. I didn't mean it.

Yes I did, said Sarah. But I'll take it back if you want me to, Charmion.

Charmion dabbed at her eyes with a corner of Sarah's blanket.

Okay, she said. Sniff. If you take it back. Okay. This time.

The thing is, she said, you just don't know. I have to forgive you because you just don't know.

We don't know what? I said.

Wearing a ring is serious for us, said Charmion. Wearing a ring means something. Pledging your trust means something.

Who's *us?* I said.

Mormons, said Charmion.

Oh, Mormons, I said.

Mormons are real serious people, said Charmion. We don't pledge our trust lightly. I really mean to stay faithful to Claude all summer. She said.

Oh, God, said Sarah, falling spread-eagled onto her back on the bed.

All summer: she said.

Well. We laughed at Charmion but in our hearts we were jealous.

She wasn't even cute: Charmion. She wore glasses. She had chalk-white skin and reddish freckles. She had fits. She was only seventeen. She looked like Little Orphan Annie. How could it be that she was such a mutt, and only seventeen, and already had a boyfriend; and me and Sarah hadn't so much as a sign of one? Where was the justice in that?

It entered our file—mine and Sarah's—of major beefs against God.

There was a boy in my life, though: I lied. It was just that he didn't count. I thought like this in those days: that if it was happening to me, it wasn't any good. Couldn't be. I mean (this is old-hat psychology, but I'll tell you about it anyway) I honestly believed—not in my head, but in my heart, in my head I thought that I was God's gift to the intellectual world, an Albert Einstein—I believed in my heart that I was the mutt of the century. Compared to me, Charmion was Marilyn Monroe. Sarah was Garbo.

The name of the boy who was in my life was Michael: a first-class name, I couldn't get around that. No hick name there. But otherwise pretty much of a mutt. Nice: don't misunderstand me. He was one of my favorite people, one of my dearest friends on earth. I liked him enormously. But he liked me too; or I was pretty sure he did. Therefore he didn't count. You can see how that would have to be true?

Who does Michael belong to? asked my friend Ellie (who had been my freshman English teacher the year before and who qualified therefore as older and wiser) when she stopped at our table in Shevlin Hall on the U of M campus one noontime when we were having lunch. Is he yours?

Well, I said. He's everybody's.

You sparkle when he's around, she said. You come to life.

Oh, I don't, I said.

You do, she said.

Well. He's not mine, I said.

Is he Carol's, said Ellie.

No, I said.

Sarah's?

No.

Then he's yours.

No. I said.

Certainly not Beth's.

No, not Beth's, I said. I laughed: he doesn't like Beth at all, I said. I don't think. Nobody likes Beth.

I'm telling you, said Ellie. I know about these things. He's yours.

Ellie, I said: Michael is not mine. Not. Mine.

Have it your way, said Ellie. He's not yours. But he's a darling.

He is? I said. Astonished. Michael?

Michael. She said. He's adorable.

Adorable.

For heaven's sake.

IX

Back to Mimi, the dormitory maid.

Actually, you know, there was absolutely nothing wrong with Mimi. She was just an ordinary person—so far as any of us knew—trying to do her job. Her job was basically to keep the halls and common space in Canyon girls' dormitory clean, and to report on whatever went on to the dorm matron, Mrs. Mason. We saw her as a Quisling, and Mrs. Mason as the Gestapo.

This business about the can of worms had a sort of basis in fact: Mimi's face, perhaps from the sun, was deeply browned, and was very wrinkled, very lined. But she was young, sort of young, maybe thirty or thirty-five, and she had a nice figure. She dressed well when she wasn't wearing her uniform. She had her hair done in West once a week and it looked super. Really. There was no reason to hate her.

There was a lot more reason to hate Mrs. Mason. *Her* job was to keep order in the dorm and ride herd on all of us, enforce the curfew, etc. When we were at work, she was our supervisor. But as a matter of fact we didn't hate Mrs. Mason. We were afraid of her. Mrs. Mason had some sort of presence, some personal power, that Mimi didn't have, and so Mimi was chosen. For what? Why, to be hated, of course. Someone has to be hated. Has to be. That is clear.

After the incident with the bottle—which Mimi and Mrs. Mason believed was deliberately aimed at Mimi, I can't imagine how they could have come to that idea, because the chances of the bottle even breaking that heavy glass were very slight, much less achieving a deliberate trajectory; Beth's arm must have been fantastic that night, World Series quality—anyway, after the bottle incident, things calmed down for a while. We were replete with our success; and also we were scared. We laid low. We thought we had, you know, used up our luck.

As someone, Sarah maybe, said, we had gone perhaps a little too far . . .

Sidney was contemptuous of the whole affair, but she was grudgingly admiring of Beth's part in it.

I never thought she had it in her, she said.

I thought Beth was chicken to the core.

She's not, I said. She's very brave. I always knew that.

Still, it was a stupid thing to do, said Sidney; you guys are all incredibly stupid.

And to toss it right at Mimi, she said. You might as well say you tried to kill her, she said. What the hell have you got against Mimi?

We didn't aim it at Mimi, I said. It was an accident. That it came that close to her.

Still, she said. If you'd thought of it, you'd have aimed at Mimi.

Well, I said: I guess. Maybe.

What have you guys got against her? said Sid. She seems like a fairly decent sort, I mean she's no worse than anybody else . . . reasonably okay . . .

A decent sort, I said: Oh. No.

Well, what then? said Sidney.

I don't know, she's the dorm maid, I said. Isn't that enough?

No it isn't, said Sidney.

Charmion hates her.

Sidney snorted. I hate Morelli, she said: I don't expect you to hate her.

She's ugly, I said.

So what? said Sidney. I'm ugly.

No you're not, Sid, I said.

Yes I am, said Sidney.

I looked at her. Well, maybe a little, I said. Maybe a little ugly.

Maybe a lot, said Sidney.

There's a difference, I said.

What difference?

We *know* you, I said. Besides, you don't look scared.

Sidney laughed. You guys are so dumb, she said.

She put her arm around my shoulders and gave me a half-hug. Dumb old Pooh Bear, she said. Dumb old Joan.

I felt honored above anybody.

X

My memory of West is that it was on the very northmost edge of Yellowstone. But that can't be true, can it, because it is called West? It must be on the west edge. My memory is wrong.

But in any case, it was a one-evening trip. We could leave Canyon about 5:30 p.m., right after supper, and be back by midnight or one a.m. We could either drive in with one of the people who had a car, or we could hitchhike.

Either way, it was a one-evening trip.

There were other places we went that summer too. Cooke City. I forget why we wanted to see Cooke City. There must have been a special reason, there was always a special reason. Cooke was an overnight trip. We got there in the evening and found a church and slept on the church pews and checked out the town in the a.m. and hitched back that afternoon.

Virginia City was a whole weekend. Virginia City was a ghost town. It was restored just like it was back in the old days of the frontier; I remember a dummy in a chair in the window of a barber shop, and the red and white striped pole in front; but no people really lived there, like nobody lives in a museum. Virginia City was like a museum.

(Unless it was Cooke that was the ghost town, in which case I don't know why we went to Virginia City. You have to remember that all this was more than thirty-five years ago now.)

And there was also Jackson Hole. Jackson Hole was pretty close, just a day trip, but it was probably the most important place of all to visit. Sidney said that we *must not* spend all summer in Wyoming and miss Jackson Hole; in fact for Jackson Hole she made a special exception to her otherwise iron rule and went with us.

We went on a day when Beth was scheduled to work, because Sidney wouldn't go if Beth came. Does that sound mean? Well, it was mean, of course it was. But that's what happened anyway; Sarah and I both would rather have Sidney than Beth. So Beth got left.

We felt guilty, Sarah and I, of course we did: but not guilty enough to try to change anything. Well, you must know how that is?

Sid kept talking about Jenny Lake all the way to Jackson. Jenny Lake this and Jenny Lake that. Wait til you see Jenny Lake. But she wouldn't tell us what was so fabulous about Jenny Lake.

What's so great? we asked.

Well. Its. She said.

I can't tell you.

Let it be a surprise. She said.

And the Teton Mountains, which were at Jackson too. Or Jackson Hole was by the Tetons. Actually, the Tetons were another reason for going to Jackson; Sid said we absolutely had to see the Tetons.

And Sid was right: the Tetons were wonderful. Jenny Lake was wonderful.

Here was this dusty little western town, I mean what the hell, *this* is the fabulous Jackson Hole? and we walked up this rise in the ground and over the top of the rise and there it was. Jenny Lake, I mean, *there it was.* Pop! It was the suddenness that was so stunning. There you were walking up this dusty rise and then you are on top of the rise and you look down and ah! there is the lake, set in grass like a round sapphire. No beach or shore—just green grass and then the blue lake. It was like the earth had an eye, and the eye was looking at me: absolutely clear and open, and absolutely mysterious. Because it just *looked* like you could see into it; you couldn't really. It seemed as though you were seeing to the depths; but you weren't really. And I wondered: what could the depths be?

The Tetons, too. What is it about the Tetons? They are better than other mountains, more wonderful—everyone who sees them agrees on that. I think there are three of them: the Grand Teton and Moran Peak and one other peak that I can't remember the name. But that doesn't make a whole lot of sense, because there should be only two, because teton is an

Indian word for *breast,* the Tetons are supposed to be like the breasts of a woman.

So maybe it was only two mountains.

On the other hand, I once knew a woman with three breasts: honest to God.

The summer we were at Yellowstone, the big news was that there had been a plane crash near the top of Moran Peak early in June, before we got there, and no rescue attempt had yet been made. Sid knew all about it.

Right there, just above the saddle of Moran Peak, she said. The wreck is still up there.

They say you can see it if you look really hard, she said.

Oh, come on Sid, that's got to be twenty miles away, said Sarah: or more,

No, but the air is so clear here, in twenty miles there is nothing to stop your seeing, said Sidney.

Sid: Don't you see that long sort of smudge there right near the top of that level place? with that kind of dot?

Me: Well, maybe . . . I see . . . something . . .

Sidney: Well, that's supposed to be the plane. That dot.

Sarah: Why haven't they gone up there yet?

Sid: You can't go up there except just at one time of the year, any other time you will start an avalanche . . .

Me: When will they go up?

Sid: Next year. I guess. Some time. I don't know for sure.

Sarah: How many people were there on the plane?

Sidney: About sixty . . . a convention of bankers and like that . . . they say there was a million dollars on the plane . . . and jewelry, tons of it . . . and it's finders keepers . . . whoever gets up there first gets it . . . that's the rumor around here . . .

Treasure, said Sarah.

You bet, said Sid. And how.

Are they sure they are all dead, Sid? I asked.

Oh, my, yes, said Sidney. She squeezed my arm. Silly old Pooh, she said. Sure they're all dead. Someone would have lit a fire or something. If they were alive. No one could be alive up there any more.

Sarah was staring at the peak. Her eyes were full of distance. *It's too beautiful* . . . she said.

How, Sal? I said. How too beautiful?

It's too beautiful for anyone to live up there. Maybe God could live up there. Not people. Not money. Not a broken airplane. Said Sarah.

Then we all looked out across twenty miles and were silent at last.

XI

One evening, just after supper, Charmion came running into my room to find me. Hey, Joan, she screamed. Hey, there's somebody here to see you! There's a *boy* here to see you!

Impossible, I said.

Well. I honestly could not imagine who it was. I honestly did not think for one second of Michael.

He's out in the front, she squeaked.

You have to remember how bored we were. A visitor—anyone's visitor—was a change, a gift from God for all of us. Nobody hogged a visitor for herself. Himself. Visitors were common property. We all got a piece.

I followed Charmion along the second floor hallway and stepped out with her onto the little balcony above The Lobby.

I looked down.

Michael.

My God.

I didn't see just Michael. You have to understand this. I saw home, I saw safety, school, someone who knew me at home, someone from the dearest place on earth, someone from Minnesota: a flat place, that I dreamed about at night, a place where there were no mountains. Home.

I thought my heart would simply burst with joy. Michael, I said. I flung my arms wide in welcome. Then I held my arms down to him in an ecstacy of sudden affection. Michael! I shouted. Michael! My God!

How wonderful to see you! I cried. It's like a vision! Where did you come from?

He smiled at me, darling Michael, and I guess that split-second is the closest I ever came to falling in love with him.

And then the hordes descended:

Hey! Introduce us!

Who's your friend?

Hey! Want to come to a party, cutie?

And the moment was gone.

When I got downstairs and outside, Michael's little brother, John, who was sixteen, was with him. It turned out that they were taking a trip across the country with their parents and their sister Mavis, and Michael and John had dropped the others off at Canyon Lodge, and had come over here just to see us. Me? No, no. All of us.

Let's go out tonight, I said; I'll find a girl for you, John.

God, Joan, Michael said. He'll be your slave for life if you can do that. That's the first time anybody has ever treated him as if he were a serious adult . . .

Michael laughed: that familiar, dear laugh—amused, superior, a little nasal.

No problem, I said.

It wasn't as easy as I thought it would be, though; when I tried to find a girl for John I ran into extreme prejudice.

Sixteen! shouted Charmion. You are seriously asking me to

go out with someone who is only *sixteen?*

Well, you're only seventeen, Charmion. I thought it would be perfect, I said.

Well, it isn't perfect, said Charmion. It isn't even okay.

Please, I said.

No, she said.

I'll be your slave, I said.

For how long?

A whole day . . .

You are asking me to break my trust, Charmion said. You are asking me to betray Claude.

Oh, well, Charmion, you said it yourself, I said: John is only sixteen, so he doesn't count.

Claude would think he counted, Charmion said.

Please, Charmion, I said. Please do it, please, please, please . . .

Please.

Please.

In the end she agreed. She took me for two dollars; a Nut Goodie; my pink sleeveless blouse; and a day's slavery.

It turned out to be a real date.

After we introduced everybody and talked and all, Michael and John took me and Charmion to dinner that evening in the Canyon Hotel dining room. I had never eaten there before—as a matter of fact I had never even been in it before.

Sidney was our waitress; I requested her specially.

Will he tip? she asked.

Of course he'll tip, I said.

(Leave a big tip, Michael, I said at the end of the dinner. It's the done thing around here.)

Later, we sauntered around the grounds of Canyon Hotel. I showed Michael the few good sights: Upper and Lower Falls, Yellowstone Canyon, and a dear little creek that flowed near the hotel, landscaped with stepping stones and some kind of water flowers and a little rustic foot bridge.

John and Charmion disappeared for a while; we thought they had gone off for good but we had no such luck. As it turned out they stalked us and giggled and chattered about us all evening. The Love-Birds, they called us.

The Love-Birds! Well, you know, we might have been. Michael drew confidence, I guess, from the night and the summertime, and he put his arm around my waist as we walked. He never did that at home. We went out onto the little footbridge and stopped and leaned over the rail of the bridge and talked and dropped sticks into the stream. There was romance in the soft velvet night. The stars were so close, so close, as they always are in the mountains.

And I actually forgot to be hostile. I was actually, well, almost nice. Nice-ish.

The moonlight poured down and made everything magical. It changed Michael's face, which I normally thought of as comical, to craggy and rugged. And there was just a second when I thought: If he wants me . . .

Hey, Love-Birds! came a call out of the night from the high bank above us, at the top of a flight of stairs.

Oh, Jesus, said Michael.

You better be careful, Love-Birds! Charmion's squawk pierced the night: There are bears out tonight . . . bears were seen just upstream from here . . . five minutes ago . . .

Is that true, Charmion? I yelled.

Wouldn't you like to know . . . ?

John and Charmion hooted and giggled above us and their young, young voices drifted down and echoed in the gully, and hung over the water.

Know . . . know . . . know . . . ?
Hahahahahahahaha . . . ha . . . ha . . . ha . . .

Goddamn little pests, said Michael. I'm going to tear John's ears off tomorrow . . .

* * *

We came up the stone steps and out of the stream bed into the harsher light from the windows and yard-lamps of the hotel. No romantic evening was worth meeting a bear; and it was possible that it was true that the bears were out. There were always bears roaming around the hotel grounds. They came and raided the garbage cans at night. Grizzlies, brown bears, all kinds.

XII

In the morning, very early—maybe 4:30 a.m., before I went to work—I saw Michael and John off. We had breakfast together first, this time in the hotel coffee shop.

This is awfully expensive, Michael, I said. And last night.

Oh, well, said Michael, with the high-pitched, careless tone in his voice that made me laugh every time he used it: It's only money. He said.

Easy come, easy go.

I knew what he did to get money. He worked evenings and Saturdays in a music store in Minneapolis, and then on Sundays he was an organist in Salem Lutheran Church. And he went to school somehow in between.

Hey, big spender, I said; and caught his eye; and we both laughed together.

Yeah, he said. Laughed: huh, huh, huh.

We went outside, into the early morning, and Michael and I watched while John loaded up the Ford four-door.

The first rays of the sun just broke over the faint crests of faraway mountains. Suddenly everything turned to gold in the golden light.

Irene was out already feeding her squirrels. I saw her over by the stand of trees where she always went. She stooped and held a nut in her hand and one of the squirrels came right up to her and took the nut out of her hand.

See that woman over there? I said. That's Irene. She feeds squirrels all the time. In fact, she's our resident looney.

Michael looked where I pointed. My God, he said. Oh my goodness.

What's the matter? I said.

That's my aunt, said Michael.

Your *aunt?*

Yes, my mother's sister, he said. My Aunt Irene. My God.

I saw that he was serious.

You are kidding me, I said.

No, no, he said; that's really my Aunt Irene.

Well, listen, I absolutely couldn't stand it. That's an aunt? I said.

That's an honest-to-God *Aunt? Your* Aunt?

Why, I simply went to pieces; I gasped and choked and giggled—ha-ha, ho-ho—at the idea of our squirrel lady being an aunt. Anybody's aunt. But Michael's aunt: it was too much, too *too* wonderful . . .

Michael grabbed me and sort of choked me. Shut up, you dope, he said: she'll hear you . . .

Finally I stopped.

It's not that funny, said Michael.

Yes it is, I said: It really is that funny, Michael. I'm sorry . . .

Aunt Irene is kind of crazy, Michael said. I guess you know that. She believes . . . things . . .

They say she comes here every summer, I said. Charmion says that's crazy all right.

Well, my God, said Michael; I don't know why I forgot that she would be out here. Well. I do know why. We never think about her. We never talk about her. I just forgot about her . . .

Does she live in Minneapolis? I said.

No, she's from Flint, Michigan . . . oh, my God . . .

He seemed so upset.

Are you, um, all right, Michael? I asked.

He laughed. His laughter floated high and a little hysterical in the stillness of the early morning world.

Am I all right? he echoed.

Well, of course! Certainly!

What's Hecuba to me? he said. Laughed. Huh, huh, huh. That high, hollow, nasal laugh.

Sophisticated.

It's embarrassing, though, he said. You know.

Well: I suppose: I said. Maybe.

Although, I said. Sidney says Irene is okay, Sidney says she isn't hurting anybody . . .

Oh, my God, said Michael. He laughed again. He clapped a hand to his head. Just what everybody wants, he said: to have an aunt about whom the best thing that can be said is that she isn't hurting anybody . . .

Well, I said. Do you want to go over and say hello?

He stared at me.

Are you kidding? he said.

I guess so, I said. I looked at him in the dawn's early light, and the gold had dimmed, and I saw that he was really a pretty homely guy. A mutt, in fact.

I guess I am kidding, I said.

XIII

Irene is Michael Leland's aunt, I said to Sidney when I saw her next.

I know, Sidney said. She told me.

Did she know he was here? I said. And John?

Certainly she knew, said Sidney. She's just a little missing in the upstairs. She isn't blind. She isn't deaf.

He didn't think she knew, I said.

Certainly she knew. Said Sidney.

Was she hurt, that they didn't, you know, that they didn't say hello?

I said.

I guess so, said Sidney. Probably. Well—maybe. I don't know. Maybe she expects that. She didn't exactly sound hurt. She sounded more . . . amused, sort of . . .

We were standing outside of the dormitory, by the Lobby door, and we could see Irene at her usual station, over by the stand of trees off to the right of the dorm, between the dorm and the hotel, feeding the squirrels again. Michael's Aunt, I mean: I saw her now as Michael's Aunt. Suddenly one of the squirrels jumped right onto her hand and walked up her arm and sat on her shoulder.

She laughed, and the wind brought her laughter to us: clear, gay, delighted.

Saint Francis, I said. God. Saint Irene of the Squirrels.

Michael says she believes things, I said.

I know all about that, said Sidney.

What does she believe? I said.

Well, see, said Sidney. It's kind of touching, Pooh Bear.

She put her arm around my shoulder, like she did sometimes, dear old Sid, and we stood that way and stared at Irene. Michael's Aunt.

Touching? I said. Sid? To you? Not to you . . .

Oh, I can be touched, old Pooh, said Sidney: I am not so tough, I feel things . . .

Well, sure, I said. I didn't mean that you didn't feel things . . .

I know what you meant, Pooh, she said. I know what you didn't mean.

Sidney moved away and sat down on the steps.

I sat down next to her.

Pause.

Silence.

Ah. Morning sun warm on my face. Bliss. Just to feel the sun. So what does she believe, I said.

Why, she's a member of some weird cult called the I AM's, said Sid.

They all believe that their souls have taken up residence in the Teton Mountains. So Irene comes here every summer, and every day that she can get off she hitches a ride to Jackson Hole and she sits by Jenny Lake and stares at the Tetons . . .

Wow, I said. That is weird . . .

I don't know, said Sid. I think it's kind of nice. I think I might be happy if I thought my soul was in such a beautiful place . . . and I could go and visit it . . . sometimes I think I don't know where my soul is . . .

Maybe in Birmingham, she said. Maybe they took my soul with them . . .

XIV

Joan, are you going to marry Michael? Charmion asked.

Marry him! I said: Certainly not.

I thought you were, said Charmion.

What in the world gave you a dumb idea like that? I said. Never. There's nothing like that between us. We're friends. That's all. That's absolutely all.

I don't believe it, said Charmion.

Don't be so dumb, I said: How come you think you know me better than I know me?

I know things, said Charmion.

Charmion, I said. Listen to me. He is nothing to me. Nothing. To. Me. Have you got that?

I was so firm that even Charmion's conceit was a little shaken.

Well. She said. I thought.

You thought wrong. I said.

Maybe, said Charmion.

But when you were so happy to see him, she said. On the balcony there. When you held out your arms: she said.

Your face was so bright. Said Charmion. You never look like that otherwise.

It was someone from home, I said.

Michael used to have a fantasy about a certain song, "September Song."

He loved that song, and he talked about it a lot. And sang it, and hummed it. Michael was a singer and an actor, did I tell you that? No, I probably didn't, because somehow that was never really part of my picture of him.

Anyway, Michael was great on that song the whole time I knew him. In the song, two lovers are separated for many years because when they are young, they somehow miss each other, they miss their chance to come together because they don't understand that they love each other. They think that love looks very different from what it really looks like. And they both marry other people, have careers, etc., etc. Then, when they are old, they meet again by accident one day, and they do understand this time, they do accept love.

Michael's fantasy was that love would happen to him that way too. In the evening of his life, he would walk into a room and see this woman, and he would sing to her: *It's a long, long time . . . From May to December . . .* and she would rise and open her arms to him . . . *And the days . . . dwindle down . . . when you reach . . . September . . .*

Folks. I am fifty-six years old, and to this day I find myself waiting for someone to come through a doorway and sing:

It's a long, long time . . .

From May to December . . .

I hear this song and I see a shadowy figure standing in the doorway.

Can you believe it? Well, believe it or not.
And I hold out my arms . . .

XV

One evening, toward the end of the summer, Beth came in earlier than usual. Her face wore a new expression—I thought there were traces of tears, but there was also: what? confidence? self-satisfaction? Something smug, in fact.

Hi, Beth: I said. What's going on?

Nothing, she said. You don't mind if I just turn in, do you?

I don't mind, I said. At all.

But curiosity got the best of me.

Is there something the matter, Beth? I said. Is there something wrong?

She stripped off her ranch pants and shirt and underthings quickly and pulled on blue striped pajamas. Of all of us, Beth was the least afraid to be naked in front of the others. Sarah undressed in the closet. I managed by undressing under my nightgown—can you believe it?

But Beth just calmly took her clothes off and put on her pajamas no matter who was there. I envied her.

Wrong? she said. She climbed into her bed and bunched the meager pillow up for a headrest. She lay down stretched out full and clasped her hands behind her head.

Not exactly wrong, she said. She laughed: that funny laugh, like she wasn't entirely in there.

More like right. She said.

What do you mean, I said.

Jay asked me to be his woman, she said. Tonight.

I thought you were that, I said.

Not . . . really, she said.

Oh: not really, I said. Oh.

He said he'd give me a day to think about it, Beth said. He

said he'll be gone until tomorrow night. He said if the answer is yes, when I come out to the corral tomorrow night I should wear a dress . . .

My gosh: what are you going to do, Beth? I said. I was fascinated. My gosh, this was the real, raw stuff. None of this September Song business. And happening to old Beth, of all people.

Was it possible to be jealous of Beth? No. This was too close to an edge. This was a corner I did not want to have to turn.

Yet. Not yet.

Some day. Not today.

I don't know, said Beth.

Don't tell Sal, Joan, she said.

I won't, I said.

Don't tell Sidney.

No. Nobody. I said.

Promise?

I promise.

I watched Beth the next day when I met her in the halls of the hotel as we worked. I watched her face for signs of the decision. But there were none. Her face was impassive as always. No clues given.

I didn't follow her or anything like that—I want you to understand this—I mean, I wouldn't want anybody to get the idea that I was terribly interested in what was going on with Beth.

But I was aware of her in ways that I usually wasn't.

I looked for her when the opportunity presented itself. I looked for her at lunch time, for example.

In the afternoon I saw her over by the stand of trees talking to Irene. Mimi was there with them too. The three of them were talking together.

In the evening I saw her go out—as she always did—to the

stables, and she was wearing her usual ranch pants, the uniform for all of us that summer.

It was very late when she came back in, and Sarah and I were already in bed. The moonlight was shining in through Sarah's window, and it fell across Sarah's sleeping form, and it lit Beth's face for a second, and her face was full of sadness.

Beth . . . I said.

No, she said: Don't.

Shut up, you guys, Sarah muttered.

And that was the end of that.

XVI

I was on the phone with Sarah one day recently—last weekend in fact—and I talked to her about this story.

You're in it, Sal, I said: and Sidney's in it. But Sid's kind of peripheral—you're really *in it*.

I *am?* said Sal.

Yeah, I said.

That's, ah, great, Sal said, sounding pretty dubious.

Beth's in it: remember when she threw the brandy bottle through the window?

Oh, do I ever, Sarah said. Old Beth: would you ever have thought she had it in her?

I put that in, I said.

My goodness, said Sal; what else? You're telling on us . . . are you telling on us?

Remember when we tied up the dormitory maid? I said. In the fire hose?

No! she said. I don't remember that.

Maybe I wasn't there, she said.

At the very end of the summer, only a few days before we left for home, the whole lot of us came upon Mimi on her knees scrubbing the dormitory hall floor at the top of the stairwell, by the little alcove where the fire equipment was kept—not far from our corner room, you could see our doorway. Beth was leaning in the doorway looking up the hall at the rest of us.

Well, look what's here, said Charmion: Old Wormface.

Mimi looked up at Charmion. Said nothing. Moved her brush in dragging wet circles.

She was dressed in her red uniform skirt and short-sleeved jacket, and was kneeling on a little knee pad. Her brown hair was, as always, arranged in an elegant do—I think she must have spent a lot of time on her hair every day. Getting it to look like that. Because she really did look nice.

Wormface, said Charmion. What are you doing here? You're in my way.

You can see what I'm doing, Charmion, said Mimi. I'm doing my job. She said.

This is a good job for you, Wormface, said Charmion. You belong on your knees. That's right for you. Isn't that right? she said, looking around at the rest of us.

We stood—me, Sarah, Connie, Brenda, and Charmion's sister Jeanne—leaning against the walls, draped on the stair railings. Beth was still standing in the doorway, looking at us from down the hall.

Right, Charmion, said Connie. Right.

Mimi stopped scrubbing and stuck her brush into the scrub pail. She straightened up, reached her hand out to grasp the railing at the top of the stairs. She tried to rise.

Charmion struck Mimi's hand from the railing. You're not allowed to get up until I say so, she said. You stay on your knees in the presence of real people.

Hey Charmion, said Brenda. What are you doing?

Charmion kicked gently at Mimi. Mimi tried to scrabble away. She slipped on the wet floor and slid ungracefully onto her side and grabbed at the pail of water and the pail of water tipped and splashed dirty soapy water onto her and in a big puddle that splashed and dripped and ran down the stairs.

I watched the water run down the stairs and whenever I want to I can watch it still: the moment is stopped in my mind in slow slow motion: the pail going over and Mimi going over and hot soapy water flowing and dividing and dripping and running, but slowly, slowly, in my memory, like thick hot syrup. I see the water run so slowly that it is like it could be put back, we could stop it and pick it up and the water could go back in the pail and Mimi could rise and walk away from us.

Humpty-Dumpty, I thought. The water can never go back, never go back.

The water.

Can never.

Go back.

That's the way it is, I thought with great surprise.

Now look what you've done, said Charmion, softly. Look what she's done, Jeanne.

See what she's done?

See?

Yeah, said Jeanne: Mimi, look what you've done.

Dumb Mimi, said Connie.

Stupido, said Brenda.

See what she's done, Joan, said Charmion. To me.

I see.

See what she's done, Sarah?

She's spilled the water . . .

Said Sarah.

How stupid can you get, said Charmion. She kicked at Mimi, harder this time, and Mimi began to cry. Boo-hoo, boo-hoo. Tears runnelled down the ruined sun-brown cheeks and ran into the pool of soapy water and Mimi's nice hair was in the water and was coming undone.

Oh, Mimi, your hair is getting wet, Charmion said. Let me fix it. Let me help you.

Charmion leaned over and yanked at Mimi's hair and the hair pins came out and Mimi's hair tumbled into the puddle of soapy water. Charmion stepped on Mimi's hair and moved her foot around and mopped at the water with Mimi's hair.

Mimi yelled in sudden pain and fear: Owww. Ohhhh.

Help me, Jeanne! Charmion demanded. Help me clean up the water . . .

Okay. Yeah. Said Jeanne.

Jeanne stooped down and grabbed a handful of Mimi's hair and scrubbed at the floor.

Ow, Mimi shrieked. *That's hurting . . .*

Is that hurting, Wormface? squeaked Charmion. Oh, is that hurting?

Do it some more, Jeanne. Said Charmion. Jeanne pulled at another clump of Mimi's hair and scrubbed roughly with it again.

Mimi shrieked: *Ow, ow, ow.*

Charmion kicked her, hard. Don't yell so loud, you crazy bitch, she said. Do you want to get us in trouble? Huh? She kicked Mimi again.

Please, sobbed Mimi. Please let me go.

My God, Charmion, Sarah said. Let her go. It's enough.

It's not enough, shouted Charmion. It's not enough, it can never be enough!

It can never be enough . . .

How can this end? Will we kill her?

Then Charmion had the great idea. We'll tie her up, she said. With what? said Brenda.

The fire-hose! said Charmion. We'll tie her up with the fire-hose.

* * *

When Mimi was securely wrapped in lengths of hose and the hose was somehow tied in a big clumsy knot, Charmion spoke to Mimi:

Wormface! she said. Look at me!

Mimi stared up at Charmion.

Listen to me. Are you listening?

Yes. Yes. Said Mimi. Sobbed. Sniffed.

Don't speak! said Charmion.

Nod yes or no.

Mimi nodded. Bump, bump went her head on the floor.

Okay, said Charmion.

I want you to understand something: said Charmion. To Mimi. And believe it: she said. You better believe me. If you ever tell anyone who tied you up, if any of us ever hear that you told, we will find you, wherever you are, and we will come, and we will kill you.

Do you believe that, Mimi? said Charmion.

Mimi nodded. Still lying in the water. Her beautiful hairdo in sad ruined loops and tangles lay in the water.

Are you going to tell?

Mimi shook her head.

All of you guys, ordered Charmion. Come around here and put your hands on the hose. So we're all in this. So nobody can tell.

Jeanne put her hands on the hose that wrapped Mimi, and on Mimi's back, and Mimi's body quivered at the touch. *Mmm:* she moaned.

Shut up, Mimi, said Charmion.

Now Sarah.

Sarah went up to the group and laid her hand on the twisted hose.

Mimi sobbed and gasped.

Sarah shivered: I saw her shiver.

Joan.

I knelt down and laid my hand on the hose. I don't remember doing it, but I know that I did it. Must have done.

Connie. Brenda.

They came, knelt, laid on hands.

Ah. Ah. Ah. Sobbed Mimi.

Shut up, Mimi, said Charmion.

Suddenly Charmion saw Beth leaning in our doorway down the hall, still watching.

Beth. You, too. Said Charmion.

No, said Beth. Her voice was soft, but it carried down the hall to us.

No.

Bitch! said Charmion.

Possibly, said Beth, and laughed.

Whore! said Charmion.

Not whore, said Beth. She laughed her light, mocking hollow laugh.

Bitch, perhaps, she said. Whore—no.

My misfortune? she said.

Then she disappeared into our room and the door closed softly behind her.

XVII

The very last day came that I was, we were, at Yellowstone Park; and we each had our interview with Mrs. Mason, and she gave us our check for what we had earned all summer. They didn't pay us at all until we had stayed and worked the whole summer, see, that was part of the deal, I suppose otherwise some people might have gone off early and left the hotel staff short-handed.

Mrs. Mason also gave us our final evaluation for the summer.

One by one we—my crowd, I mean—went into Mrs. Mason's office, and one by one we came out, and each of us in our turn looked a.) amused as hell and b.) fairly shattered.

You know what she told us? She told us that she couldn't prove anything but that she was as sure as she could be that we were behind everything bad that had happened all summer at Canyon Hotel. She blamed us, for example, for Edgar Bergen's luggage getting lost. And a whole bunch of other stuff.

And she said she was going to put the whole lot of us on a list of people who would never be allowed to work again in any national park in the whole United States. Ever. Blackballed, she called it.

So I stand before you: revealed as one who is forever blackballed from the national park system in the U.S.A.

Later that day, when everybody else was packing, I walked by myself up the road, maybe half-a-mile long, that led to Upper Falls. Actually, I went around to various places to say goodbyes. Upper and Lower Falls, the canyon, etc. I went alone, because I needed to be alone to come back to myself. You know what I mean. I needed to prepare for going home, where I would be a separate person again, and not a member of a crowd.

I carried with me up the road the thought of having been blackballed.

Blackballed. Me. The good student. Etc. Etc. What an idea. So *funny*. Who would want to come back here anyway? Ever? Who would be that crazy?

Blackballed.

It felt terrible.

It felt, you know, like justice had been done.

Yes. Truly: justice.

I walked along the road to Upper Falls carrying shame that would never leave me, never end, I thought.

I met Irene on the road. She was coming down from Upper Falls and I was going up. I had my eyes on the ground, pretty much, and I didn't see her until she was right there in front of me.

Good morning! she said. Sang. It's a beautiful morning! Her voice was like bird-song—light-hearted and airy, happy and chirpy.

She stopped in front of me. And I stopped.

I'd never been that close to her before, you understand. I'd never spoken to her. Why would I? Why would anybody seek out a crazy person like Irene?

And suddenly, you know, something funny happened. Strange, I mean. When she said it, the morning *was* good; it *was* beautiful. My eyes locked on hers, and her eyes were this absolutely clear blue, like the blue of Jenny Lake. Pop! Like that. Like Jenny Lake with the sky and the mountains in it. Bright blue.

She put her hand out to me. I took her hand in mine, it just happened as easily as breathing, and we stood that way for a long second. She kept smiling in this absolutely cracked way, this, this *happy* way, and she held onto my hand and I couldn't take it away, and I couldn't not look at her, I couldn't look away, and I couldn't take my hand away.

Then she said this crazy thing to me.

You can change, dear, she said. People can change.

They can? I said.

Yes, she said. They can. They do.

She laughed: a fantastic trill of pleasure.

And her laughter was innocent and knowing, like a child's laughter, and I guess she saw something very, very funny somewhere because she just stood there and laughed and laughed, holding my hand all the while, just threw her head back and got into it, and I can hear that laughter still, and after a while when I hear it my memory of that laughter can fill my sad and separated heart and it can bounce—ping! ping!—off every little tiny green leaf on the trees that edged the road to

Upper Falls and it can fill the whole world: and when I let this happen, when I let my memory go like that, pretty soon it is like I also know something *so funny . . . so strange . . .*

She must have changed. She couldn't always have been a feeder of squirrels. A dweller in the Tetons. Maybe once she was a teacher. Maybe she was a clerk in a hardware store. Maybe she was an artist. A shoplifter. A traffic cop. A murderer. A maid. Who can know?

And one day she changed. Or, over many years she changed. You don't have a kid in kindergarten saying to herself: Well, now, I think I'll grow up to be a feeder of squirrels. That couldn't happen.

Maybe only miracles can happen.

XVIII

The next morning, early, we got on the train that would take us back to Minnesota. Home. More home now than before: for me, anyway.

Me and Beth and Sarah and Sid. The others, of course, we had to leave; they were going in the opposite direction, their home was somewhere else.

I boarded the train feeling dejected and exhausted, after a restless night of little sleep. The others looked as bad as I felt. Except Sid. Sid looked okay. Well: why wouldn't she? *She* hadn't done anything wrong.

She was very mad at me and Sal and Beth, and she sat with a couple of her other friends toward the back of the car. I suppose she knew what we had done, though I never knew for sure. We never talked about it. Ever. Dear old Sid, she had been blackballed along with the rest of us. Guilt by association.

I shared a seat with Sarah, and Beth sat alone across from us and a couple of seats back, looking out the window.

We just sat that way—or leaned and tried to sleep—for hours. Into the afternoon.

So boring. I sat and doodled with a pencil on a piece of paper: You Can Change, Change You Can, You Change Can . . . You. Can. Change.

U
CAN
CHANGE

Like a, what do you call that kind of poem that makes a shape on the page? Something . . .

And I folded my piece of paper over and over, twisted it and folded it in my fingers: a fragile promise of redemption.

Finally: I'm hungry, I said.

I'm not, said Sarah.

Beth?

No.

I said to Sarah: Do you want to watch for the last of the mountains?

No, said Sarah.

Okay, I said.

I looked across and back at Beth, and I saw slow, difficult tears slide one by one down her face.

Beth: I said softly.

No, she said. And turned her face to the window so I couldn't see her tears any more.

And so we all went home again after that summer: each of us finally and more clearly separate from one another than we had ever understood before.

THE ITALIAN STORY

Whenever I think about that time, the image that always comes into my mind first is of the mountains, far off, dim, almost indiscernible in the distance; and then, beyond that far range of mountains, another range, even dimmer, more distant yet—do I really see them? well, maybe, or no, maybe not—barely seen, barely shadowed out of the distant, muted sky.

And I am sitting on a marble bench by a shrine at a crossroads in Italy, looking at those mountains, waiting for my daughter, who has gone down one of the roads that cross here: waiting for Margaret to come back and save me.

Will she come back at all? Well, of course, why shouldn't she, heavens, she is not that tired of old Mum. Yes, but what if something happens? You never know what can happen in this world. The world is a very dangerous place—I have lived long enough to know that. . . .

I have lived long enough: that phrase echoes and echoes in my mind. I have lived long enough.

Well, that was in a way, you know, the point I came here to make. It certainly wasn't to travel: I hate traveling. I love my home. I carried along in my suitcase one of my famous recycled envelopes—I am heavy into recycling and into efficiency; maybe, now that I think of it, they are the same thing—anyway, a 9 x 12 manila envelope labeled "for Margaret" and containing a whole bunch of stuff having to do with my death.

I feel that I am, in the matter of my death, an advanced thinker, way ahead of most folks in this crazy American society. I absolutely believe in preparing in advance for the event; and I brought along copies of a) my will, b) my power of attorney, for health care and for financial affairs, you have to have two forms, if you can believe it, nothing is simple any more, c) my living will with the requisite instructions, d) headstone and grave arrangements in Lakewood cemetery. Etc. Etc.

Yeah, well, that's good, said Margaret. That you brought this stuff. I think it is absolutely essential that we should discuss this stuff before you go home. . . .

That's my girl. . . .

Once when she was little, Margaret said to me: Mom, are you afraid to die? Afraid! I said: Certainly not. I'm looking forward to it. . . .

Honestly. And that kind of set the tone for future discussions.

Not a real good answer for a child, I realize now, probably realized at the time; but then, I was not a real good mother.

Not in any classical sense.

Why can't you dress like a mother? said M. to me once. You don't dress like a mother.

My goodness, I said: what exactly do mothers dress like?

Well, they, uh, they wear dresses, said Margaret. And they wear aprons. And real shoes.

I see, I said. I looked at myself: jeans and Grateful Dead T-shirt. Worn tennies. Christ. I can see that I am the world's worst.

Well, Margaret, I said. You pretty well have to take what you get in this world. And in God's great grab bag, you got me.

Basically I like you fine, Mom, said my daughter, probably about ten at the time, earnestly. Whenever she talked to me seriously, she went into this terribly earnest mode, for all the world as if she were the mom and I the child.

Sometimes I think she *is* the mother; I *am* the child. Just before I came on the trip to Italy with her, I had a dream: in the dream, our friend Vange—who died last spring—talked to me on the phone: It's time for you to come with me, she said. Was I scared? Not one bit. Gosh, thanks, I'd love to, Vange, but I can't, I said. *My mother still needs me.*

I told Margaret about the dream. *Your mother!* she said. How about *me?* Don't *I* still need you?

I figure the dream means you, I said. I figure you are the mother.

She looked at me funny. Well. Wouldn't you? If your mother said that to you?

Well, whatever. Margaret said. Just so you don't die yet. Not right away or anything.

There was some more of the dream, and I am telling it to you now because it was kind of funny. And because it stays with me. In the dream, Vange said: on the phone: Hey, I didn't think of that. And: Wait right here, I'll go and see if I can change the plan. So I hold the phone in my hand for a while and then suddenly two guys come, dressed in black overcoats and black hats, looking—honestly—like FBI men, and they are angels, and one takes my arm on one side and one on the other, and they say, okay lady, come on, we've got to go now, and I say, No, wait, Vange is looking into this, Vange is going to get the plan changed, and one angel throws his hat on the ground in a great huff and says: That woman! Always messing up the arrangements. . . .

Anyway, Margaret said, I'm certainly glad that Vange decided

THE ITALIAN STORY

to change the plan. I'd miss you, old Mum. I'm not ready for you to go just yet.

I believe she wants to think of me as terribly brave and strong. I think that is the image she formed of me in her childhood years, after the divorce; and anything that happens to threaten that image is frightening. At least it seems to me that is the way it works.

The image was never altogether real, but how is she to know that? I was never very brave. I was never very strong. I was making it on nerve alone in those days; and I have to say, looking back on it all, that I did have that: nerve. But I figured she needed to believe that I was brave and strong, and so that's what I said I was. And she believed what I said. Some place in the heart's core she believes it still, I think.

Once I said to her: Margaret, how come you've got such a chip on your shoulder? How come you race out of your corner with your dukes up every time?

Mom, she said. I learned that from *you.*

Well. That hit home all right.

Margaret! I said. Laughed: I couldn't help it. It had its comic aspect once I saw what had happened.

I was wrong! I said. I made a mistake! Goddammit! Stop! Change! Now!

I know what she means, though. One day in the fourth grade at Marcy school she came home sobbing. Mom! she said. They took me out of Miss Merrill's class.

Why did they do that? I said: quietly, but feeling like I could become dangerous.

They said there were too many of us in the class. . . .

I crouched down in front of her on the kitchen floor. I was so angry. I remember the linoleum as clear as day. Brown speckled it was, so as not to show dirt, and awfully beat up.

In those days I could still crouch; I don't know if I could today. In those days I didn't think I'd ever get old either. In those days all I knew was that you had to come out fighting or you'd die. They'd kill you.

Margaret, I said. I will go over to the school tomorrow and I will fix it. You will be back in Miss Merrill's class the next day. I promise.

I absolutely promise.

How will you do that? said Margaret, nine years old, grubby, sniveling and snuffling. Christ. When she looked like that I wanted to kill somebody. Anybody.

I don't know, I said. I'll think of something. Believe it, kid. *I will fix this.*

Will you go and see Mrs. Mullins? she said. Sniff, sniff.

I'll see Mrs. Mullins, I said.

Mrs. Mullins was the principal at Marcy.

Oh, I'll see her, I said. I'll fix Mrs. Mullins' little red wagon for her, that's what I'll do.

The next day I went to the school and met with Mrs. Mullins in her office. I explained the whole thing: divorce, learning disability, favorite teacher, etc., etc. Very logical and polite I was. Pleading my excellent case.

Finally Mrs. Mullins said: I agree with you. The child should stay with Miss Merrill. And she will. She'll be moved back today. But I have to tell you that you gave me a bad day, she said. I met your daughter in the hall this morning and she said: Hi, Mrs. Mullins, my Mom is coming over here today and *she is gonna raise hell!*

So you see? How it all happened?

Oh, my.

Sorry, Mrs M. I said it then and I'll say it now. Sorry, sorry, sorry, I'm sorry.

THE ITALIAN STORY

But on the other hand, without learning that scrappy, fighting way, how would Margaret ever have been able to cross all the barriers that were in her path to get to where she is now? How would *I*?

Sitting on the marble bench at the crossroads in Italy and staring into the far distance at those faint layered mountain ranges, I can think about . . . oh, things . . . anything.

Mountains: did you ever read a book when you were a child called *The Little Lame Prince?* By (I think) Miss Muldoon. Are you that old? Could anybody write anything these days under the name of *Miss Muldoon?* It's, you know, just out of the question, isn't it? Well, when I read it, I thought it was very sweet, that it was by Miss Muldoon; and I loved the story, I read it over and over, it was about a sad little boy, a prince, who was crippled and who could not run about and play like other children; so he stared out of his tower window at The Beautiful Mountains—that was their name, The Beautiful Mountains, like you would say The Rockies, The Alps—off in the distance, and, I don't remember, did this happen often, or only once? anyway, his velvet and ermine cloak curled up at the edges and became a sort of flying boat and carried him off to The Beautiful Mountains and I thought, Oh! I want to go there, oh, take me with you, I am sad too . . . I am crippled too. . . .

But I never got to go to The Beautiful Mountains, no, I had to learn to live my life, one way and another.

I'm not crippled, you know. Not in any usual sense. I am, to be sure, in a fair way to become that now that I am getting older: what with arthritis, tendonitis, plantar fasciitis (no kidding) and what-have-you.

But I think, you know, that "crippled" meant "hurt" to me then, and maybe still, *hurt* in some hidden part of the spirit, some place where all of us are alone and scared stiff.

Crippled. I thought I had better explain or you would get the wrong idea. About me. I am only crippled in the same way you are, in my human heart.

I stopped being *Mom* and became *Mum* when Margaret went to England as a student at the AA, which is the Architectural Association. *Mum,* she called me in her first letter, and then explained: That's what people call their mothers here: *Mum.* Cozy, don't you think?

Mum. Hm.

I wrote back and signed my letter *Mum.*

I like *Mum,* I said.

I never liked *Mom.*

And thus I became Mum. Thus accidentally things do happen to us. Thus accidentally Margaret went to England, and loved it, and stayed; stays still. Seeks now for British citizenship, which she says will give her freedom to move around in the whole European community, freedom to work anywhere in the EEC. (That middle E means Economic. European Economic Community. I suppose you knew that.)

It'll be good for me as an architect, old Mum, she explained.

But. I said. You'll have to give up U.S. citizenship. Surely U.S. citizenship still means *something.*

No, she said. I mean, no I won't give up U.S. citizenship. I can have dual citizenship. Then if I want to I can work in the U.S.A. too.

Hm. Okay I guess. I said. Grudging, though. I was.

Listen, don't crab at me. I know she had to grow up and leave me. But it's hard when your only darling lives four thousand miles away and is busy as a biscuit and you see her maybe every two years.

No wonder they say: Don't put all your eggs in one basket.

She'll never come back here to live, says her father, my ex–, even glummer than I am about it.

It's good for her as an architect, I say. Prim and righteous. Quoting M. I understand her, he doesn't, I think.

Oh, as an *architect*—he snarls. She's a *woman*. She should be getting married, she should be giving me grandchildren, *that's* what's important. . . .

God, you're so old-fashioned, I said. How did you get to be so old-fashioned?

Yes, well, he said.

Such a fuddy. I couldn't stop. I always battled for her against him. He wanted to protect her. Let her go, I said. Let her try. Let her be what it is in her to be.

Her biological clock is running out! he screamed, in that whispery scream he had that used to drive me crazy.

Listen to him, I said.

Biological clock.

Indeed.

I remember once when Margaret was about two years old; she had a favorite activity, she would stand up in a sturdy old rocker we had in the living room and she would rock like mad, full-tilt, like a trick rider in the circus, like a knight-crusader riding full out at the infidels. Gadunk, gadunk, the old rocker would go, hitting bumps in the floor.

One day Bud saw her doing it. You are letting her do that? he screamed. He grabbed her off the chair and hugged her. A *baby?* My god!

She could fall.

She could hit her head on the fireplace.

She could get killed.

And: How long has this been going on?

Oh, about six months, I said.

Well, it's going to stop now. *Never* let me see her doing that again.

Okay, I said. Yassuh, Massa.

And quit this Massa stuff.

Okay, M . . . Sir . . . I said.

Christ. I must have been awful to live with too. After all, he really believed that she would get hurt. And I really believed that a) she wouldn't and b) it's better to get killed than to grow up afraid.

On the day after Bud moved out when we were getting the divorce, Margaret rode a bicycle for the first time in her life. Before that, Bud always thought it was too dangerous at her age. For god's sake; she was eight years old. How old do you have to be? Twenty? Sixty?

She got on the thing, an old one I got at a yard sale, but quite sturdy, and she wobbled on down the street, wobble wobble, like any other kid, but doing all right as far as I could see. And I followed, wringing my hands . . . oh, god, she'll fall; oh, god, if she falls Bud will blame me. . . .

She didn't fall. She didn't fall.

And twenty years later she was the only woman architect who went up on the scaffolding on the outside of Westminster Abbey when they were restoring it, about nine years ago; she went up there to draw the gargoyles so the sculptors could make new pieces from her drawings to repair the original broken gargoyles. Can you see it? My daughter, in her black architect's suit, they all wear black, I don't know why, but they do, my girl a mile up on that splendid old pile. . . .

Margaret, I said. On the phone. If you could get me a snapshot of you up there on the scaffolding, I believe I could die happy. . . .

Oh, *Mom*, she said.
You know how they get.
Oh, Mom . . .
For heaven's *sake. . . .*
And I never did get my snapshot.

I laugh inside of myself at Bud. Such a fuddy-duddy. What has he to do with *biological clock?*
What's Hecuba to him, or he to Hecuba?
He's, you know, right, though. I hate to admit it. Isn't he?
Goddamn it. You can't have it all. You really goddamn it can't have it all. The kid and the candy-jar syndrome: *Let go and you can have your hand back. . . .*

Sitting on my marble bench, looking out over the mountains, remembering Miss Muldoon and the prince, I think: how did I get here? and where is here? Some place called San Vito d'Altivole. I think. Near Montebelluna. The sign on the front of our bus: *Montebelluna.*

Montebelluna. Couldn't that mean "Beautiful Mountains"? Something like that? Think about it.

Pull yourself together, I say. To myself. Firmly. You got here on a bus. Before the bus, a train. Before that the waterbus in Venice.

And after every other form of transportation, when the bus stopped, turned left on the road where we needed to turn right, feet. Ordinary human feet. It was the feet that gave out. It was the feet that betrayed me.

Betrayed? Once again, get hold of yourself here. . . .

Walking, walking, walking, on a dusty road in Italy: suddenly over a slight rise, round a slight bend, a bench and a shrine appeared, and a house, kitty-corner. *What's that?* I said. Well. Nearly sobbed.

A *shrine,* said Margaret.
A lovely little shrine.
A *bench,* I said.

I am the one who, visiting London eight years ago, when I was only fifty-seven, dreamed up—out of dire desire and deep need, even then—a great title: "Benches and Chairs of Britain."

I told you I was a bad traveler.

But five will get you ten that there's just as many of me out there as there are of the other kind; and I'll bet anything you want that "Benches and Chairs," properly marketed, which almost nothing is these days, except maybe Tom Clancy, people like that, would be a bestseller.

I can't say "runaway bestseller"; you can see that.

Margaret is a traveler, has been all over the world. I am dumb with admiration. Not envy, you understand—admiration.

I envy no one.

Except maybe that guy over there who has found a better bench.

I admired Margaret for example when she took her portfolio and got on a plane to London, went to the AA, and got accepted into their program just like that. Into the most prestigious school of architecture in for god's sake the whole world. She couldn't get into any graduate school in the United States. She tried a lot of them, Harvard, Stanford, Columbia, and was turned down; her GRE scores were pretty bad, well, I told you about her learning disability. They have another name for that now, but a rose by any other name, etc. This is what it comes to: there is no written, timed test anywhere that she can pass, and no job anywhere that she can't do. Or won't be able to some day.

That's how good she is.

So my kid went to the AA.
America's loss, England's gain, the way I see it.
Am I proud?
Oh, folks. Fit to bust. I am: me: old Mum.

The whole thing with the train and bus trip started in Formosa Square in Venice. We were bumming around Formosa Square because it was close to home and I had—yeah, right—sprained my ankle the day before and I couldn't go far. There I was, walking down the hall coming from our room, and the whole hotel was riddled with booby traps, steps up, steps down, no pattern to it, no rhyme or reason, as there is no rhyme or reason to any part of Venice, and whoa! down I go and smash my head on the wall and turn my ankle stepping off of one of the booby traps.

Mom! Mom! yells Margaret, and crouches down by me. Are you all right?

In the clutch I guess she forgets that I am now *Mum*.

Give me a minute, I say. I'll let you know.

I laugh. Am I hysterical? Well, I am embarrassed, of course I am. What a dumb-ass American thing to do.

The maid is there too. Blah-blah-blah, she says, la Mamma . . .

Yes. Definitely la Mamma. And the rest might as well be Greek. It might as well be Sanskrit.

The maid is a middle-aged sharp-faced black-haired woman; I thought of her as a harpy until I fell in her hallway and all of a sudden she is sweetness itself. I sit there on the floor, tears running down my face, from shock, I guess, not from pain, I feel nothing yet, and the maid kneels down beside me, yes, on her actual knees, and she smooths my hair back from my face, over and over, pet pet pet, and wipes my tears away with an end of her apron and sings and croons: Mamma . . . la Mamma . . . dum de dum de blah blah. But soft, soft, sweet.

I want to crumble on her skinny breast. I restrain myself, however, even in this catastrophe.

Thanks, thanks, I say. Bun jorno. Whatever.

Listen to me now, folks: Go nowhere without learning the language first.

Grazie, grazie, says my daughter.

How's your head? she says. To me.

It's not my head, I say. It's my ankle.

I heard your head crunch, says M.

Yeah, well, forget about my head. I've sprained my ankle. I say.

Head, what is a head? You don't have to be able to think in Venice. You just have to be able to walk around.

Ask her if they have an ice pack, I say.

The maid, I mean.

M. says something to the woman, who still pets my hair back from my forehead and croons.

And who now jumps up and runs off.

She's getting one, Mum, says M. We are back to Mum, the immediate emergency is apparently over.

Anyway, that's the way it all starts, and the next day and many ice-packs and an ace bandage later there we are in Formosa Square.

It was Monday, our fourth day in Venice. Margaret deposited me by a fountain in the square and went off to something called the Biennale, which is an international fair for architects held every other year: hence, Biennale, or two-yearly-event. We did not plan to be in Venice for the Biennale, but it surely did come in handy when I went out of commission.

Go ahead, I said to M. I'll be all right here.

You sure? She hovered.

I'm sure.

And she went.

I *was* all right. For the first couple of days in this city it seemed to me that they had completely overdone the water thing, but after that, Venice got to me. It dawned on me that the boats, which serve as trollies or buses, public transportation, were after all not so terribly slow. And—a day later, maybe—I saw something else: slow is fine. Fast is crazy.

But then came the real discovery. This is what it is: that whatever I choose to look at in Venice—is beautiful. Everything about Venice is beautiful to look at. The color of the dirty water in the canals—is beautiful: green, bright, opaque, like a gel, not sparkling, no, but shining, glowing, smooth and deep; like frosted green grass. The broken and chipped old walls—are beautiful. The ancient paving stones, the houses, the boats, the bridges, god, are beautiful. There is a door in Venice—a for Christ's sake *door,* only a *door* in a back street—before which Margaret and I one day stood and gaped for quarter of an hour; not a door to a cathedral, you could understand that, but a door to an ordinary house, not even a very grand house, and not even an old door, a new door for heaven's sake.

Well. I am trying to tell you that a simple door in Venice was a great experience, almost an experience of worship; and everything else was just as good. By the time I landed in Formosa Square to sit by the little fountain I was dazed, amazed, with so much beauty, dazzled, confused and agape. This is true, I swear to you: I had to kind of slit my eyes, so that my eyelids were drooping, only about half open at any one time; with any given glance I saw only half of the available view—it was as much as my eyes could tolerate.

Was it the light? Did some strange quality of light make everything beautiful? Maybe. Maybe that was it.

When I shall come to die, I think I might like to bypass heaven and go to Venice instead, and maybe be a door, or a stone, or a drop of green water.

Every scrap of matter there, I think, may be inhabited by souls, by angels, who made the same choice.

Maybe Vange could arrange it for me. Maybe the FBI angels—remember them? in my dream?—could, properly directed by dear Vange, pull that off for me.

I have such thoughts in Venice. Nothing seems impossible there. Everything seems sunny, even when it is raining.

Mum, says Margaret. That green water you're talking about is basically shit.

Yeah, well, I say. I know that. I say.

Well. Believe it or not, after a while, an hour or so, I got tired of sitting by my fountain and being dazzled; human beings can get tired of anything, even Paradise; so I got up and limped off to explore the periphery of the square. I found a little bridge that went across a tiny span of water, a little, little canal, a ditch, really. The bridge was new, absolutely modern, wood and brass, sleek and simple; and it crossed the green water to an ancient building; and it was so cunningly made, that bridge, that neither was diminished, the new or the old.

Just then Margaret got back—it seems the Biennale was closed on Mondays. She read the sign on the building for me: the Querini Stampalia. A museum; restored by an architect named Carlo Scarpa, who was also the designer of the bridge.

Let's go in, says Margaret, and so we walk across the lovely bridge, Japanese in its simplicity; and inside we look around a bit, and everything is as smooth and sleek and simple as the bridge; and we watch a movie about this Carlo Scarpa and find that he has indeed been influenced by Japanese design.

On the soundtrack of the movie we hear Scarpa say: blah blah blah: which translates: I need a pharaoh; and then we hear that he found his pharaoh, a very rich man who let him build a whole cemetery for him—the rich man—and his wife, a great tomb.

Gosh, I'd like to see that, says M.

Well, why not, I say. Where is it? Can we get there?

Architects are important people in Venice. It seems that the city, built on little islands, jumping from one island across to another, and extended out over the water of the Adriatic, the Lagoon of Venice, on pilings that have lasted for centuries, it seems that the great city is sinking into the sea. And her architects busy themselves these days with the question of how to save her.

Margaret, as a student, got caught up in this problem. In her first year at the AA, her whole class went to Venice and the instructor presented them with a building in one of the out-of-the-way little squares; there it is, he (or she? why not?) said: Figure out a way to save it.

Margaret took me to see that building; it looked to me just like everything else in Venice: old, pretty decrepit, leaning to one side, and beautiful.

What was your solution, I asked her.

Well. She launched off into a very technical dissertation on stresses and what-have-you.

It reminded me of the time I asked her father—on the day we got married, if you can imagine it—how the hydrogen bomb worked.

You're not getting it, are you, Mum? said Margaret.

Well . . . not exactly *getting,* I said. I mean, I'm *interested,* truly I am. . . .

It's hard stuff, old Mum, said Margaret. Kindly.

It is strange and in a way rather wonderful to have reached a point in life where your kid has to be careful not to talk down to you.

Once I said to my own mother, when she was getting older and I was having to take care of more and more of her affairs:

Mama, how does it feel all of a sudden for me to have to act like the parent and for you to be the child?

Well, she said, it doesn't feel good. . . .

No, it doesn't feel good. But on the other hand it doesn't feel real bad either. Actually, there's something kind of comic in it. Was it the Greeks who thought that comedy more truly represented life than tragedy? and was a higher form?

Maybe it was the Romans. As you can see, my classical education has a few holes in it.

Romans were early Italians, weren't they? Or Italians are the descendants of Romans? Am I wrong about that? I wonder if I am wrong about that. I will have to ask Margaret. She will know.

Carlo Scarpa, according to the movie, had solved the problem of the sinking city primarily by not fighting the encroaching Adriatic, but by accommodating the sea instead. He accepted as a given the idea that there would be floods; and then he built his first floor, his ground-level floor (water-level?)—in the Querini Stampalia and in other buildings that he restored—as a sort of sewer, honestly, a sort of drainage-system/museum.

All of the exhibits, of for example books and drawings, rested on high tables, and the tables and the floors were made of marble or some such substance that would not be hurt by water; and when the floods came, water would slosh on the marble floors and around the marble table-legs and never reach the exhibits.

And around the edges of every room, at floor-level, were built marble troughs, drainage channels, little canals, that would carry the water out easily and efficiently when the water receded.

I was simply speechless with admiration: so simple.

You'd just mop the floor up—slosh, slosh—and there you'd be—ready for business again.

Like I said before: a sort of sewer.

All of the design elements inside the building were as simple and clear as that idea, as clear and clean and lovely as the bridge outside; and the old and the new lived together in peace and perfect harmony.

Margaret says it wasn't marble, it was something else, but I have lost the paper I wrote it on. Marble will have to do.

Save me. Remember that I said on the first page of this story that I was waiting for Margaret to come back and *save me?*

You know, in one way I am—have been—wondering what the hell I meant by that, it just popped in more or less on its own, and things that just *pop in* are usually quite important, and have to be accommodated and understood, like the floods in Venice—otherwise you lose the core of the story, its true heart, the place where it really touches you; and in another way I know perfectly well what it means.

It means that I was abandoned on a marble bench at a crossroads in a foreign country where I didn't know the language and I was very scared, that's what it means.

We were on this bus, finally, that brought us to the fork where the road turned off to San Vito d'Altivole, which was the town that the map showed as closest to the cemetery. The turn-off was maybe three miles back from my bench. Margaret had tried to make the bus driver understand what we wanted: I mean, Margaret knew enough Italian to get along under ordinary circumstances, *How much?* and *Where is the toilet?* and like that, but this was harder.

Cemetery—of Carlo Scarpa—near San Vito—where is? . . .

After a while the driver gets the drift, more or less. He nods and grins in triumph. *Ah!—cimitero—si, si.* . . .

He chatters away, smiling and waving his hands.

A woman on the bus who speaks some English tries to rescue. He says there are two cemeteries, she tells us.

He says the one at San Vito is too far for you to walk, more than six kilometers, a long walk, too long, he says there is one closer, very near, you should go to that one. . . .

Margaret says: One cemetery is as good as another?

Yes, says the woman. He says the nearer one is just as good.

You've seen one, you've seen 'em all, I say.

Mom—says Margaret.

Oh, yeah. You know what *Mom* means, don't you? It means Shut the Fuck Up.

Okay, I said. Okay.

He says he doesn't want to let you get off, says the woman. He says there is no bus from here. He says it is too far for you to walk. Me, that means, folks. Too far for *me*. I mean, she looks at me when she says it, she looks me over, up and down, and I know it is me she means. The old lady. Me.

Nonsense, I say.

I'm a good walker, I say.

Margaret looks dubious. I know she is thinking about my ankle with the ace bandage wrapped around it.

The bus jolts to a stop.

There is a great commotion. Everybody tries to talk at once. The driver chatters a mile a minute. The woman tries to interpret. Margaret tries to talk to both of them.

I say: I'm getting off.

I say: Of course I can walk.

I rap on the glass panel of the door.

So finally the driver points the way down a road to the right, *blah blah six kilometers,* he says, but he does open the door, we are not after all his prisoners, and I step down into the dust of the road and I turn and say—I have learned this much—

THE ITALIAN STORY 89

Grazie. Grazie.

And we step down off the bus onto a narrow gravel road that almost certainly will not take us to any civilization.

Unless to the civilization of the dead? *Cimitero?*

Could you call that a civilization? Sure you could.

You may, if you are clever, or wise to the ways of scribes, have thought that I am thrashing around here just a bit. And you are right, that is just exactly what is happening, I am thrashing around. I am like a fisherman with too many lines out, I am running from one line to another, looking to see if the big fish that I know swims here somewhere is nibbling at any of the lines.

The shrine, the bench, the crossroads, the mountains, the manila envelope, the fall in the hotel, the *cimitero,* the bus, *The Little Lame Prince,* the floods in Venice, all lines, thrown out by me more or less at random, into holes where a fish might be lurking.

I know that this fish is a big one. But can I land it? Is it too big for me? Where am I going? What does it mean? All writers are fisherfolk, and they all—if they are really writers—ask themselves such questions: *Where am I going? What does it mean? Will God give me the story?*

Sometimes there are no answers.

But sometimes there are.

Sometimes they land a big, big fish: a real story.

I'll bet you never saw a storyteller thrash around like this before, did you? But they all do. If they are any good at all. If they tell hard stories. They just don't let you see the thrashing, that's all. There is a rule somewhere that says thrashing around shouldn't show.

I never cared for rules myself.

I knew someone once named Jo, who, when I was complaining about how hard it was to write a story, leaned back and said: sighed, breathed: Well, if it's so hard, why bother?

Yeah. Why bother? Do you see what a job I am doing for you here?

So we sat down, Margaret and I, on the warm marble bench in the soft sun of Italy and sized up the situation. It seems to me that I have walked at least three or four miles, and my ankle—remember my poor old ankle? it has never been given much of a chance to recover—my ankle is hurting some, and is threatening to give out altogether.

We sit quietly for a while and stare out at the mountains.

I wonder what those mountains are, Margaret says. Could they be the foothills of the Alps?

I don't know why not, I say. But what do I know?

Look, I say. There's a second range behind the first one, if you look very carefully.

You can hardly see it. But it's there.

I see it, says Margaret.

Right then is when I remember The Beautiful Mountains. Do you remember The Beautiful Mountains? I almost say to Margaret, and then I realize that she can't remember that, she can't remember any book from her childhood, not even books that were read to her, she was so afraid of words on a page that she would twist out of my arms and run away when I tried to read to her.

She would listen to songs, and poetry that I had memorized: that was all.

I don't think I should try it, Margaret, I say. Meaning the rest of the walk to the cemetery.

I don't think I should go any farther.

I mean, it isn't as if we know where the cemetery is. It isn't as if we could say: one mile more. I say.

It could be a mile. It could be five. We don't know. It doesn't seem to me that I can take the chance. I say.

You go, I say. I'll wait for you. I'll sit here on the bench.

You wanted to see it too, Margaret says.

I know, I say. But I'm sixty-five years old. I've seen a lot, I don't have to see this too.

I don't like to leave you, she says.

It's okay, I say.

I'll be okay.

You're getting old, Mother, she says. Looks at me funny. Accusing.

Aren't you?

I am, I say. Yes.

Mother. Oh, my. We are in deep shit now. I can see that.

I *will* be okay. Won't I?

So she went. She left me sitting alone on my marble bench like a lump on a log. I watched her stride away down the dusty country road, long, capable strides, a good walker, off toward the mountains at first and then, when she was past the kitty-corner house, turning where the road turned, walking along—look at her, I thought, look how she walks, so strong, so tall and proud and healthy, I used to walk like that—there she goes, almost out of my sight behind the kitty-corner house now, almost gone, my beautiful girl.

Margaret *is* beautiful, you know. But she doesn't seem to know it, and in a way that adds to the effect. She has thick auburn hair, God knows where she got that, her father's is black, a throwback to a long-ago American Indian ancestor, and mine is brown in its original state, gray now; M's hair is cut short these days, I think perhaps in an attempt to look like an architect. Architects appear to have a sort of dress code, a grooming code. This is not a joke. All architects look the same. All of them that I saw in England, anyway. They all wear black, all the time as far as I can tell. It's like they are all trying to say: *Don't look at me, I'm not really here, I don't count, no, look at my design, look at my building, my building is what counts.* Honestly. It's like what they *do* is more clearly what they *are* than in any other field that I can think of.

And then there are, you can understand this, practical aspects to the whole thing. It's like wearing a uniform, I would think. When you wear a uniform, you don't ever have to puzzle about what you are going to put on. The whole problem is removed from your life. And when the uniform is all black, things are even simpler: you can, for example, just throw everything in the wash together. No sorting, no worrying about Will This Fade? so what if it does? I mean, I admit that no one has ever explained this to me, I admit that I am just making it up, but this is what it looks like to me, an outsider.

It is as though they have simplified existence in every way possible, so that they can just Do This Thing, which is ever so much more important than they are as people. I believe they really do to some extent think like this. And they work so hard—the fact that my daughter could take a whole month off just to be with me, I took as an enormous tribute to *me*.

Gee, I think to myself, she must really like me. Old Mum.

Mum. I can't tell you how that delights me, how that *charms* me.

Some more about architects and their code. Margaret had a dinner for me in her flat in London—well, Jason's flat, actually,

Margaret lives with Jason and Susannah; Jason is a composer of very modern operas and Susannah is another architect—M. had a dinner for me after we got back from Italy. Everyone who came to the dinner, all of Margaret's friends, were architects, except one, Frances, who was married to an architect: Stephen, who sat at the other end of the table, far from me.

I sat next to Frances.

I think it was planned that way, don't you? Somebody for me?

Frances said: When I married Stephen, I had to learn a whole new language. I mean, listen to them. . . .

So I did listen.

And by god, they could have been talking Sanskrit. (I know that Sanskrit is no longer a spoken language, give me some credit here, but you know what I mean.)

It's like a religious cult, said Frances. I mean, I try. I do try. But it's almost impossible to break in. It's almost impossible for me, ever, I think, to be anything but an outsider. . . .

Can this marriage be saved? I say to myself. But inside of myself, of course, I mean; I'm not that much of a fool.

And suddenly I see why my daughter does not marry. She is married already, as I am married now to these words.

I think of Vange, who said many times that she thought Margaret would probably not marry. Vange was our friend who died just this past spring; remember, I told you that, and I told you about the dream with the phone call and the FBI angels; anyway, Vange died on March 25, two months exactly from her seventy-eighth birthday, not so old, seventy-eight, not really old enough to *die.*

It was like abandonment, when she died, it was simply outrageous. I mean I certainly never thought she would, and certainly not *then,* not so *soon.* . . .

We (me and all her other friends, lots of us) were thinking

about what nursing home to put her in when the time came, for god's sake, we were thinking *nursing home,* that was god knows bad enough, we weren't thinking *death.* . . .

She lasted for five weeks after she had a brain hemorrhage—a mammoth subarachnoid bleed, one of the nurses said, and I overheard, I wasn't supposed to hear that, I was a layman, layperson, and not a member of the holy priesthood, I wasn't supposed to be told anything, god, it sounded so terrible, how could I get along without Vange? she was my oracle: *Vange says Margaret won't marry, Okay, I believe it, Margaret won't marry.*
Vange says that's Okay, all right, I believe that too.

They wouldn't tell us whether she was going to die or not: We just don't know, they kept saying. She could wake up tomorrow and be right as rain. We hope for a full recovery. They said.

Yes, and I hope for world peace in my lifetime.

I didn't know whether—or when—to tell Margaret. I mean, gee, if there's all this *hope,* and I knew Margaret would drop everything and come, all the way from London to Minneapolis, and what if it was nothing, well, I mean nothing *really,* what if everything was going to be okay after all?

Vange was far more than just a friend to Margaret, you see. Vange was the person who taught Margaret to read. I told you that M. had a learning disability? Well, when I met Vange, Margaret was eleven and still couldn't read, I mean there she was, this talented smart child, and locked inside her own head because she couldn't master the symbology that lets us transmit an idea from one mind to another: if you can't read in this society, Christ, you are up the old creek.

And Vange taught Margaret to read.

Once I came upon Margaret—when she was back home, visiting in Minneapolis—reading my copy of *Heart of Darkness.* Not just *any* book; no, a *hard* book.

Reading it for pleasure.

I had to leave the room, I was crying suddenly for pure joy and gratitude.

Sometimes Margaret fusses about not having produced a child or children. She too worries about her biological clock. Once she said: it's sad when I think about it, I mean, here is this tree, and this branch that is me, and it will end with me, there will be no further branch, no flower, there will have been no reason and no purpose for the branch that is me . . . .

Think of it another way, I said. Maybe you *are* the reason. Maybe you *are* the purpose.

Maybe you are the flower.

How long do I have to be goddammit *grateful* to Vange? I said once to a friend. I mean, it feels so *heavy,* it feels like such a terrific burden. . . .

For teaching Margaret to read? said the friend—forever, that's how long. . . .

Forever.

Sonofabitch.

I was, though. Grateful. Forever. To the end. Beyond. Even now.

I guess you could say that Margaret is an architect today because of Vange. I guess you could say that Margaret is alive and okay today because of Vange.

I had an attack of sanity after about a week and I did call Margaret and Margaret did come and she was mad as hell at me for not calling her sooner, but the way I see it things worked out exactly right: Margaret got there just in time to have a rational dialogue with Vange, a day when Vange seemed herself and like she might be going to get better; and then she fell into a coma and never waked from it again in this world, and Margaret saw that too, and understood that Vange might die.

If she had come earlier, she would have gone home again thinking that Vange was going to be okay. As it was, she said to me before she left, Margaret said, I mean, not Vange—Vange left us no last messages, she left no will, no power of attorney, and it all fell on me and her other friends, there were no relatives; and it was so hard, such a godawful mess; and that is why I made a will and all the rest of it and why I wanted to talk to Margaret about it all—anyway, before she went home, M. said to me: Mom, I understand that Vange might live and she might die, and I see that whichever way it goes will be okay . . . .

So you see why I think that it all worked out in the best way possible even if Margaret was mad at me.

Once when M. was about ten years old, right around the time when I was getting the divorce from her Daddy and going to graduate school, she came up behind me in the kitchen while I was standing at the stove, stirring some made-from-scratch vegetable soup, one of my specialties, I remember all this because this moment is burned into my cortex or wherever total amazement goes: M. came up behind me and kicked me in the back of my leg as hard as she could.

I was too astounded even to react like a normal person, hit her with the spoon or something.

Why did you do that? I said. Quite quietly, and holding the wooden spoon over the pan.

Because you won't let me kick the cat, Margaret said, and I gotta kick *somebody.*

Yup. We all gotta kick somebody. And there goes another line dropped into a likely-looking fishhole.

* * *

So anyway, about five pages back there I was sitting on the marble bench and Margaret was walking away down the dusty gravel road between San Vito d'Altivole and the Carlo Scarpa cemetery. Folks, I go haywire inside when I think of that soft, soft September landscape, soft sun, twisted olive trees on distant hills, autumn wildflowers growing by the road, the sweet shrine, the mountains: only one thing foreign in all that landscape: me.

I can *see me* in my mind sitting on the bench; and the object I call "myself" is so alone, so strange and so alien in that picture.

Well. Things began to happen. Things do. This crossroads was marked on the map as a town, San Vito, and kitty-corner from the bench and the shrine was the house that I told you about before, and after a while a man came out of the house. He sat with me for a while on the bench, chatting a bit, mostly smiling, a wonderfully exaggerated grin that I assumed was an attempt to bridge the language gap; he knew I wasn't getting it; but he was doing his absolute damnedest, and honestly, I was appreciating it like crazy; and then he asked: *Coffee?* Blah blah blah *coffee?*

I'd love it, I said. Grazie. Smiled. Nodded.

Grazie.

He went back to the house and disappeared inside the front door. This house, by the way, which is called a town on the map, is sitting all alone in the middle of nowhere, opposite from my shrine. Maybe I said that before. I forget things.

I have been sitting here for a long time, it is *my shrine* now, it is *my bench*.

The nice man—dark, curly hair, maybe thirty, very good-looking, M. and I have been commenting since we got to this country on the beauty of the Italian men—he comes back with a small china saucer and a very ornate little glass, a treasure, and in it is hot strong sweet coffee, I don't like the coffee much, but I drink it anyway, and I smile and smile.

My face feels like it is going to fall off. My face feels like it is made of plaster.

Somewhere in back of my face is a terrified person who is yelling: What if she doesn't come back? What if I am left here forever? What if I never get home? Oh, home, home, home . . . well, you know the litany.

The man takes the glass and the saucer when I am finished.

Grazie, grazie, I say. I smile. Oh, do I smile. And he smiles too. He goes back to the house.

I think that what happened next is that somehow the word went out that there was a crazy old foreign woman sitting on the bench by the shrine. That is the only way I can explain the people who came. Unless God sent people to try to talk to me. I like the God theory, but a lot of folks don't. A lot of folks will reject my story out of hand if I try to push the God theory. So maybe there was a telephone, and the word went out on the telephone.

Though I have to say that I did not see any wires or telephone poles.

In any case, after a while, half-an-hour, maybe, I have lost all sense of time sitting here on my bench, after a while a young woman rides up on a bicycle. Hello, she says. Oh, my. I am so happy to hear that one word in my own language: hello. I suddenly remember—now, while I am writing the story, not then—I remember an old Russian woman that I used to feed in a nursing home in Minneapolis, U.S.A.; her name was Sonia and she was completely alone, no one spoke a word of Russian. One day I called a Latvian friend who spoke a little Russian and he taught me to say: *dobre utro:* something like that: which—I believe—is good morning. Hello, Sonia, I said when I saw her next: dobre utro. Why. She grabbed my hand and kissed it, she went completely nuts, she chattered away, cried, so happy she was to hear that one word in her own tongue.

Do you speak English? I say. To the girl on the bicycle. *(Oh, please . . .)* A little, she says. I have been to the University where I studied English a little. But that was—um—a week past?—a year past. . . .

Do you need some help? she says.

Oh, no, I say. Thank you. You are kind. But my daughter will come back soon.

The young woman looks baffled.

My daughter, I say again. Something from God knows where jumps into my mind. *Mia figlia,* I say.

Her face clears.

Si, si—figlia. . . .

Mia figlia—has gone—I point—up that road to see a cemetery—*cimitero*—which was designed by one of your great architects . . . Carlo Scarpa. . . .

Oh! she says, illuminated suddenly. *Scarpa!*

God. I am *understood.* I am not just twisting in the wind here. I have spoken a name and someone recognizes it.

Scarpa. God bless.

My daughter—*mia figlia*—is an architect. . . .

Oh, an architect—si, si—wonderful, a wonderful thing. . . .

But it doesn't last. She doesn't stay. Of course not, how can she, she has things to do. She gets on her bike and wheels off, back in the same direction from which she came, toward the mountains.

Then an old man comes. He is also on a bicycle. His face is brown and deeply lined, weathered by sun, maybe, wind, who knows, maybe he has been on this bicycle all his life, has been beaten up by wind and sun all his life; he is very old, older than me, eighty at least I should think, but he looks just terrific, marvelous, tough as leather, hale and healthy.

Maybe he is a grower, maybe he belongs to those olive trees in the distance, maybe . . .

He gets off his bicycle, props it on its kickstand, and holds his hand out to me. I take his hand, it is warm as the bench on which I am sitting, warm as the sun.

Buon giorno, he says.

Good day. Yes. He smiles.

I smile. Buon giorno, I say. See: little by little I learn.

Apparently he speaks no English.

He waves his hand in the direction of the mountains, toward the olive groves. It seems to me that he might be telling me that he comes from over there, that he lives over there.

I come from the U.S.A., I say. Minnesota.

Oh! *U.S.A.!* he says. Bella, bella. Smiles. See? U.S. citizenship *does* mean something.

What are those mountains? I ask.

Are they the Alps? Are they the foothills of the Alps?

Ah—*Alps*. He laughs. I have said something silly. But I don't care. He still holds my hand. At home I would have wondered what the hell he was doing. Here I can feel kindness flowing from his hand, I feel a little bit—yes, I know this is, what they say, Over The Top, but I am a stranger in a strange land, every little crumb helps—I feel a little bit *loved*. Yes. Honestly.

Or, if you can't buy that, *accepted*. I feel *accepted*. And—*lord*—acceptable.

He releases my hand, but gently, as one would set down with care a teacup.

He points to himself.

Uno, he says. He holds up one finger.

One. Yes. I get it. I nod. I hold up one finger also.

He points to me: *due*. Holds up two fingers.

Yes. Two of us.

Then he holds out his hand to me again, and I put my hand in his.

Uno, he says. One.

Then: *Alps,* he says. No. And he says a word: the name of the mountain range, I think, it starts with M, Mum-mmm. Mumbledy. Something like that.

I say it after him: Mumbledy. He smiles, Si, si, he says. Mumbley-mum.

Oh, lord; we are communicating.

He releases my hand, goes to his bicycle, kicks the stand back. He gets on and pedals away, back the way he has come, the same way the girl went.

Buon giorno, he says as he leaves.

Buon giorno, he calls back over his shoulder. His white hair ruffles in the wind made by the moving bicycle.

Buon giorno, I call. Wave.

Good day. Good day. Yes, have a good day. It is a prayer, isn't it. Have a good journey. Have a good life.

One.

The shrine. Margaret's *lovely little shrine;* I should tell you something about it. It is built under a tree, up against a tree. Lord knows what kind of tree; I have never been good at such details. My memory of it is that the shrine rested on a square stone base, about three by three feet, wide, deep, and high—well, maybe a little higher than wide and deep—and was encased in glass: a glass cube, again maybe three feet square, again maybe a little taller than wide. Over all was a pitched roof of wood shingles. Inside the glass cube stood a statue about two feet high of the Virgin Mary—not the Madonna, but the Virgin alone with her hands lifted slightly and spread in blessing.

On the bottom of the shrine, just around the statue's feet and out to the glass, was a velvet cloth, dark red, and placed on the cloth, here and there, were what seemed to be offerings. There were a few pieces of money, silver coins, lira, I suppose;

a fresh rose just beginning to droop in the heat, lying at the statue's feet; a woman's watch, still—I checked—keeping good time, the same time as my own watch; and—truly—a cup of coffee or tea in a very small china cup, with a small saucer, both the cup and saucer doll-sized. A porcelain figure of an angel, a regular angel, not one of my FBI angels, very nice, maybe three inches tall.

I did not see how the offerings got inside the glass case, but there must have been some sort of door, an opening somewhere, maybe a hidden key, a handle I did not see. The people who lived near here must have known where the opening was; or maybe all shrines open the same way and everyone knows the secret, except strangers.

Except me: the stranger: alien.

I speculated about the offerings as I sat there on my marble bench. In my imagination I saw: a child placing the cup and saucer there: thinking, the Virgin would certainly enjoy a cup of coffee in the morning, like everyone else. I saw a young girl's hand placing the rose just so; saw her kneeling on the dusty grass by the shrine to say her prayer. The watch? oh, clearly an offering for a very large favor—maybe a happy marriage? a handsome husband? the health of a loved child? Well, you have to pardon me—a person goes a little haywire sitting alone in the sun in a strange land. A person goes a little nuts.

After a while, I said a prayer myself. It did not seem really strange to do that, not in that landscape, and heavens, I was brought up as a Catholic myself, and you know what they say: once a Catholic, always a Catholic.

Let Margaret find the cemetery, and then let her come back to me here: was my prayer. Dear Lord, let, etc. I mean, my prayer started with Dear Lord.

And—while I was at it—Lord, let her be okay in her life.

* * *

Isn't that what we all want for our children? That they should be okay in their lives? I mean, how often does one pray: Thy Will Be Done, in connection with one's child? For yourself, yes, you can take the awful risk of accepting God's will; sometimes anyway; but not for your child; never; for her, let her be okay, Lord. Let her be happy. Let her have some joy. Let her have love. *Oh, Mother Mary, let perpetual light shine upon her. . . .*

Do you love me, Mom? Margaret said that to me once, I mean, straight out you don't very often get that question. It seems to me you only get it when there's some doubt. I was so shocked, taken aback, actually, I had to think very fast how to answer it, I wanted to be so careful, I wanted to make no mistakes here: *Yes, I do,* wasn't going to do it. *Of course,* wasn't either.

What my own mother said to me wouldn't do, that I knew from experience: *Certainly I love you, you are my daughter.*

No. Not that.

So I was careful. I remember taking a deep breath: this was so important. Margaret, I said, I am damaged in the area of love. I'm not sure I know what love is. But I do know this: that if a bear was attacking you, I would put my own body between you and the bear. I know that for sure.

I would die for you: that's what that meant, wasn't it?

I held my breath.

Was it good enough? It must have been, I felt her little body—what? nine years old?—relax in my arms.

My mother loves me: oh, let her believe it, Lord. Let her know it. Even when I am gone home across the ocean. Even when I am gone from the world, across that last water. When I am dead, let her say: my mother still loves me, from the other side of death.

* * *

When Bud and I were divorced, Margaret was eight years old. We tried to time the divorce so that it would do the least damage to her: this year? next year? five years from now? when? I mean, we both tried very hard, we both thought first of her; we were not, for each other, nice people; but for her we did try hard. The only thing we wouldn't do for her was stay together. And that was the only thing she wanted.

Of course. Isn't that the way it always is? Whatever you can't have—that's what you want. The whole history of the human race is there. The goddamned apple in Paradise, for god's sake: that got us all off on the wrong foot. Or didn't. Depending on how you think in this area. Eschatology? No. That's how it will all end, isn't it? The science of last things?

So then; the opposite of eschatology: the science of first things.

Creation.

Whatever.

Margaret adored her father, and could not understand that there had to be, *had to be,* for her sake too, a divorce.

She took it very, very hard. Well. She was a difficult and unhappy child at best, and this was worst: she was angry, depressed, suicidal, profane; she had nightmares, couldn't sleep, wouldn't wash, she began to lie, smoke and steal—and Christ, she was only eight years old.

One day after her father moved out—many days, day after day—she stood in the middle of the living room of the apartment on Eighth Avenue and Thirteenth Street near the University, the apartment she and I moved into after the divorce, and screamed. I tried to put my arms around her. She fought my arms and scratched and bit: and screamed.

I tried to get just a little closer to her, just a little closer. She screamed me away.

Finally I just gave up and stood at the edge of the room and watched and listened while she screamed and screamed and tore at her clothing and swore: Motherfucker! motherfucker! bastard! fucker! bitch! cocksucker! and there was nothing I could do there was nothing I could do there was nothing I couldn't even touch her God help me oh God help me

until finally she fell in a heap and slept and I left her there, I put a blanket over her and a pillow under her head, tried not to wake her—oh God do me this one favor, don't let her wake up—and left her lying there.

Love? You tell me what love is.

I sat down at the desk in the same room where she lay asleep and I worked on a term paper for one of my classes that was due the next day.

I was in grad school for three years. We've got a choice, Margaret, I said. We can go on Welfare so that I can stay home with you, or I can go to school so that eventually I can get a good job and take care of us myself.

Go to school, she said. I don't want to be on Welfare.

You don't even know what Welfare is, I said.

I don't care, she said. I don't like it.

Will you buy me a house? she said. When you get a good job?

I'll buy you a house, I said. If you hang in with me through graduate school the first thing I'll do when I get a job is I'll buy you a house.

Okay, she said. You can go to school.

Love? What is love? I stayed, didn't I? I went to school. I got a job. I bought a house. Somehow I made it without killing anybody. I was absolutely alone. I was so unbelievably alone.

You're doing the exactly right thing, said Margaret's therapist at Washburn Child Guidance Clinic, which at that time specialized in learning disabilities, I don't know whether they do now or not. Anyway, when I told her about the screaming incidents she said I was doing the exactly right thing.

Carol, her name was.

It all seems so long ago. Well. *Is* so long ago. Thirty years. Yesterday.

You're handling it extremely well. She said. You're doing just right. You're letting her get the rage out. You're doing just fine.

Just stand there and do fine some more. Right.

Hey: who is doing something *just right* for *me?* Who is giving me what *I* need? Who is taking care of *me?* Tears are welling to my eyes at this moment. They won't spill, though. If I know one thing from my life, it is how to keep tears from spilling.

Most of the time.

Once on the bus, coming back with Vange and Margaret from supper in Dinkytown by the University—this was after M. and I moved away from the University area, after I was working, after we'd bought the house, after we'd met Vange; and even then, when Margaret was maybe twelve, even then things were still pretty bad, but at least I had Vange then; if you buy the God notion, you'd say God sent me Vange—anyway, Margaret caught sight of a movie marquee on Fourth Street, the Campus Theater, I think it was, and the marquee said something about *Hell,* I don't know what the movie was but I know that *Hell* was in the title, and Margaret said to me: *That movie was made for you. You should be in hell;* and I found a seat on the bus somehow, blind with tears that sprang it seemed from some fountain inside, tears that poured out, not sobs, you understand, I was not strictly speaking crying, it was more like I was leaking, or bleeding. The tears just came. And came and came and came. We got off that bus downtown to transfer to a #4 bus and still there were tears; my goodness, could such a catastrophe go on forever? and Margaret was scared, Mom, Mom, stop crying, I'm sorry, I'm sorry, I didn't mean it, stop. And: I can't, I said. I can't stop. Don't worry.

And I couldn't. We are talking, like, an hour and a half, more, of non-stop leakage here.

Vange kept handing me tissues. Dear Vange.

Finally it did stop. Of course. It always stops. Whatever it is. Sometime.

Everything stops sometime. That is a core truth. Get your head around that and you'll be all right.

In San Marco Square in Venice, you can see a comic sight whenever the square floods. There are wooden supports— what are they called? sawhorses—maybe two feet tall that hold broad plank sections a few inches above the water. These sawhorses are brought out (by the Department of Floods? why not?) whenever flooding threatens, and people walk across San Marco Square, in sight of the great cathedral, on the wooden walkways.

This has happened so often that it is part of life. Only the tourists exclaim with surprise any more; or feel precariously balanced too high up; the people who actually live in Venice just accept it, pay no attention whatsoever, and, intently destination-bound, as anywhere else in the world, they go about their early-morning business. Walking swiftly with the water lapping maybe a foot below them, they jauntily swing bags and briefcases.

The flood, they know, has come; and the flood will recede.

As I said, it has its comic side: thinking of the briefcases.

And then in the afternoon the flood water will go back to the ocean and the people from the Department of Floods—I never saw them; as I never saw anyone painting a fire hydrant at home in Minneapolis, and yet the fire hydrants for sixty-five years have been nicely painted, kept up to scratch, always— the folks from the Department of Floods will take away the wooden walkways and people will once again set mortal feet upon the ancient stones of Venice.

I was talking to Margaret on the phone a few days ago, all the way from Minneapolis to London. I have found this phone deal that lets you pay only nineteen cents a minute to call London, and I am taking advantage of it while it lasts, my belief is that it won't last, you know, as I said before: nothing lasts, not even Rome, not even Venice, not even the U.S.A., we can't last either; in fact we may be down the tubes even as we speak; but meanwhile I am talking to Margaret at least a couple of times every month for maybe half an hour. Just chatting about this and that, nothing much, by far the very best kind of phone call; and somehow, in some context, I said to M: You are my favorite person in the whole world, you know.

I didn't know, she said. Really? Truly? Your absolutely top favorite? she said.

You didn't know that? How come you didn't know that? I said.

She needs much more love than other kids need, Vange said once. Well. Said many times. She needs more than you can give her, more than any one person can give her.

Yeah.

So God sent me Vange, fat old blind Vange, social worker and teacher, to make up the rest of the quantity needed, the rest of the love. And I surrendered my daughter to Vange; half, anyway; never all, oh, no, never all.

Do you love them enough to give them away, that's the question, isn't it? Do you love them enough to let them go?

You don't even write about me in your stories, Margaret

complained over four thousand miles of wire. (I know there isn't actually four thousand miles of wire, I'm not that dumb; or *is* there? How *do* they do it? But you know what I mean.)

Oh, yeah. A perpetual sore point: *How come you don't write about me?*

Because I'm too smart, Margaret. To do that. I have said for years.

People hate you when you write about them. Believe me, nobody thanks you.

But: I'm writing about you now, I said.

You are? she said.

Yup, I said. I've started to write the Italian story.

And you're telling it like it really was? she said. You're not pulling any punches?

I'm not pulling any punches, I said. I'm telling it like it really was. Or like I saw it, anyway.

I was so terrible to you, she said. I was so bad. . . .

Really? I said.

I thought you were marvelous to me. I said. And she was, you know; I mean, there she was, young and in Venice and saddled with this old broken-ankle person. Sprained ankle.

And the sprained ankle wasn't all; there was a lot else wrong with me too. I had a terrible cough, left over from a bad cold; I seemed to need a W.C. for one end or the other about every half-hour, it seemed to me that we were always following signs that said Toilet and that led from one building to another in Venice; I broke out in hives; I mean, gee, who wouldn't have been mad at me?

Under the circumstances, I thought Margaret was extremely forbearing.

Oh, no, she said. I was terrible, I was mad at you.

Like you'd done it on purpose or something.

For heaven's sake. That was not how I saw it at all.

That's not how I saw it at *all,* I said. You were great. You went and got me an ice pack and an ace bandage and you brought me a sweet little plant with blue flowers, and some cough drops, you bought me cough drops, you had to hunt all over Venice for a pharmacy that was open, because it was Sunday, nothing was open, don't you remember?

This is how it will be when I write the story, I said. I'll remember something you don't remember, I'll see something different from you, and you'll get mad.

No I won't, said M.

I promise.

Write the story.

So okay, I'm writing the story. For better for worse. For richer for poorer.

In sickness and in health. Till death.

A closer union than marriage: mine, anyway: mother and daughter. And more difficult. Fraught, if you know what I mean. Absolutely fraught.

I am very scared.

I mean, Margaret could get mad permanently. Couldn't she? Or like when I got mad at my mother, blamed her for everything, everything that had ever gone wrong, and something always goes wrong, you know that; in lives; and I was mad for at least ten years. I would die if Margaret was mad at me for ten years. I would die of grief. I would die of pain.

A year, okay. Maybe. I probably deserve a year. Not ten.

But my mother didn't deserve ten years either.

I wonder if my mother died of pain. No: not that pain anyway: because we were friends again before she died.

More or less, anyway.

Oh, gosh. What a tangled web . . . what an intricate construction is this edifice: mother and daughter.

* * *

Eventually we got back to London and had our talk about wills and death and such.

Do you want me to be cremated, Margaret? I said. Or buried?

Well I would have to say that I think that is pretty much up to you, Mum, Margaret said.

Well, yes and no, I said.

I was just horrified at the amount of money the funeral cost when Vange died. I said.

And in one way I'd rather you got the money to pay off your school debts than that we used it to plant me . . .

Plant you, she said.

Laughed out loud.

That's my Mum, she said.

I personally, for some dumb reason, would rather be buried, I said. I'd like to have, what did Zorba say? *the full catastrophe.* I mean, a wake, and flowers, and singing, and people getting up and saying nice things about me . . . and you know, a grave, and incense, and stuff . . . and stuff. . . .

And I also have this notion that unless people, like, *see the body,* they're never really sure that the person is *actually dead.* . . .

Hm, said Margaret. Can't I see you before they cremate you?

Well, I guess so. I said. If you get there fast enough. I'm assuming that you'll come for the festivities.

Mum! she said. Of course I'll come.

From the ends of the earth?

Certainly, she said: from the ends of the earth.

If you're in Hong Kong? I said. If you've got a job in Hong Kong. If you've got a job in Australia?

If I'm in Hong Kong, she said. If I'm in Australia.

If you're in *Istanbul?* I said.

Jesus, Mom, she said, what are we actually talking about here?

Well, they only keep you for seventy-two hours, I said. Then they have to cremate you. It's the law. I checked into this.

You are a very strange person, she said.

Yeah, well, I said. I am what I am.

Seventy-two hours is long enough, she said. Seventy-two hours is three days, for heaven's sake. How long did it take me to get here when you called me about Vange?—not *three days*....

Yes, well, and in some ways Vange was a lot more important to you than I am, I said. And that was right, the right thing, that she should be more important, what she did for you . . .

Oh, for God's sake, Mum, said my beautiful girl. Pushed back her chestnut hair. Flipped her chin up. Like she does.

I'll come, she said. And I'll get there in seventy-two hours. Whatever you decide. Cremation or burial.

Yes, well, it's the difference between maybe three thousand dollars and about ten thousand dollars. Seven thousand bucks would put a big dent in your school debts.

She stared at me. I could hear the word forming in her mouth: *Mom*. . . .

Like on the bus on the way to San Vito.

But: Don't die, Mum, she said. Not any time soon. I would just hate it. If you died.

She called me yesterday.

You've got a cold, I said. Her voice sounded terrible.

I haven't, she said.

Then why do you sound like you have? I said. You have too, I can hear it.

I am so dumb.

She started to cry.

I'm crying, goddamn it, she said.

Oh, I said.

Oh, Margaret, what's the matter? What's wrong? I said.

I'm so depressed, she said. Everything's going wrong, it's been raining for days, my job is so hard, the Part III classes are so hard, I can't do it, I'm dumb. . . .

You are not dumb, I said.

I would have called Vange with this shit, she said. *But Vange isn't there.* I thought: I'll call Vange. And then I thought: Vange is dead.

Yes, well, I know I'm not as good as Vange, I said. But I'm all there is now, babe.

I *do* know that I'm not as good as Vange. Not for purposes like this. Not for calling in the night when things get too hard.

I'm only good when a job has to get done. I'm what they call task-oriented.

And I'm funny. You can laugh with me at things Vange wouldn't see at all.

I'm great for the bright days.

Not so good for the sad days.

All you've got is me, babe, I said. Over the phone to Margaret in London.

So far away. So far away.

Four thousand miles of wire.

I don't like to dump all this on you, Mum, she said. I'm afraid you'll think I'm suicidal, or something.

Oh, hell, go ahead, dump, I said.

The thing is, I believe she learned from Vange's death that people die.

Well. I can hear you saying it: she's thirty-seven years old, for god's sake. She knew that people died.

Yeah, but there's knowing and there's *knowing*. If you follow me.

Her grandmother died.

Yes, but her grandmother was not that important to her, was no one she counted on to *be there*. And her grandmother was awfully old, ninety, and she was in a nursing home, and she didn't like it there, she talked all the time about how she wanted to die, she was ready to die, she was ready to go home to God, etc., etc. There was no surprise about it when she died, there was basically only relief, she wanted to go and she did.

But when Vange died it was a shock. Seventy-eight is not so very old these days. And Vange did not seem even that old, she seemed just herself, as she always had been. She was quite happy in her life, she was reasonably well, she did all the things she wanted to do, she cooked, had dinners for her friends—us—counseled people in her kitchen or over the phone, smoked her head off, unfiltered Chesterfields, for God's sake, drank when she wanted to, listened to taped books on the Talking Book—I did tell you that Vange was blind, didn't I? well, she was, she and I met when I went to work at the Center for the Blind—people came to see her, and she told their fortunes with the gypsy cards, Vange claimed to be a gypsy on her father's side, a Norwegian gypsy, if you can imagine it.

Well. What I think I am trying to say is that Vange's life was pretty good as lives go, satisfactory, and no one expected her to die when she did.

I think *she* expected it, you know; unknown to any of us, she had begun to make plans for her funeral. She had met with a mortician, picked out a casket, for example. Told him what music she wanted at her funeral. Etc. Etc. So I guess she may have had an idea that she didn't have long.

But *we* didn't know that. She didn't tell any of us. We were shocked, horrified, bereft, and pissed. She had *left us,* goddammit—now who would we talk to when the chips were down? Each other? A poor second choice.

And for Margaret more than anyone.

And when Margaret learned that people died, she learned that *I* would die. . . .

That's what she said when she was crying over the phone

yesterday—I'm afraid that you'll die too. I think you're *going to die*. . . .

No, no, I'm not going to die, I said.

I am, though.

You too.

Margaret too.

As my dear old father used to say, Margaret's grandpa, very few get out alive.

And, silly as it sounds, hardly any of us know it. Hardly any of us believe it.

It's a big secret: *we are going to die.* No one tells that secret. No one speaks of it.

And then, from my bench by the shrine, I saw Margaret, still walking tall and strong, coming along the road in back of the kitty-corner house, getting to the bend in the road and turning the corner and walking toward me. Oh, God, was I glad to see her.

Because every time somebody leaves, it is never absolutely certain that they will return. Every time somebody leaves, the little child who still lives in all of us thinks—just a little? even you?—maybe I am abandoned, maybe they won't come back to find me, maybe from now on I have to find my way on earth alone. . . .

I mean, the sudden sight of the strong young body striding along, the chestnut hair blowing, the chin up, struck into me one of those moments of perfect happiness, perfect joy: when the thing we have spent our lives waiting for suddenly happens: Lord, thanks, I am found again, once again I belong to somebody.

The Lord says: You have always belonged to me.

I say: You know perfectly well that doesn't count.

Margaret and I walked back along the dusty road. The way

back did not seem half so long—you know how that happens.

It was a wonderful *cimitero*, Mum. Margaret said. Thanks for letting me go alone and see it. I wish you could have seen it too.

She tried to tell me about how it was built, but the explanation was, well, you know, Greek to me.

Sanskrit.

I told her about the young woman and the old man, but of course, I couldn't *really* tell it. Not like it happened. Not what it—you know—meant, was truly about.

He said the mountains were not the Alps, Margaret, I said.

He said they were, um, the Mumbledy-Somethings.

The *Mumbledy*-Somethings? said M.

Yeah, I said.

Hm, she said.

And: Mum, you really are something else.

Oh, yes. I am. Angel, spirit, One. Something other than what walks here. I couldn't tell her, of course. I can't tell *you*.

I took a look back, but the mountains were gone, had disappeared into a fold in the horizon.

I think, you know, that The Beautiful Mountains were Paradise, don't you? In Miss Mullock's book?

Miss Mullock. That was the author's name. Not Miss Muldoon.

Some day.

Some day.

Let me go when it's time, Margaret.

I'm looking forward to it.

And listen, Margaret: here's my last message, my final word: Love is not a thing you feel. Love is a thing you do.

THE BOOK OF SAINTS & MARTYRS

This is a story that I have been trying to come to for more than half a century; since, in fact, I was the child I write about. The strongest image I have in my mind when I think about writing it really has nothing to do with the story. I don't think it does. But maybe it does. Since it forces its way in, like an uninvited guest, it must, in all courtesy, be accommodated, surely?

This is it: once I was on a bus in Minneapolis, Minnesota, where I have lived most of my life. A woman was carrying a little child, a baby. The child was barefoot. Suddenly the woman rang the bell to get off, and as she stood up the baby was turned toward me for a second in such a way that all I saw were the tiny soles of its feet. I was pierced with a shaft of such joy and such tenderness, fondness, that tears come to my eyes now, remembering.

And then, immediately, like part of the same memory, I think of Paulie.

* * *

Who is Paulie? You want to know? Hey. Of course you do. You want to know everything, don't you?

Like Uncle Albert, you want to know God's thoughts.

You would never have left that apple alone in Paradise, would you? No good saying: she tempted me, Eve did; Eve ate first.

You would have eaten it too. I *know* you; as I know my second self.

Paradise was never enough for us, fragile voyageurs: *More!* has always been our cry.

Give me another donut. Give me a piece of cake. Give me the next bend of the river. *Give me that apple, goddammit.* Give it to me now.

* * *

I have only one clear memory of Paulie.

I was two years old and he must have been six. I have the impression that it was his First Communion day: that doesn't quite fit, six seems awfully young for it, but maybe he was precocious at that too.

Certainly he had a white suit on. And why would he wear a white suit except for his First Communion? These were depression times in the U.S.A., about 1933 or 1934, some of the deepest years of the Great Depression; people bought nothing frivolous, surely there would be no occasion grand enough to call for the purchase of a white suit except a First Communion? or a wedding? or a funeral?

And I had on a little white dress and white shoes with straps: called, I think, Mary Janes. This would not have been quite so unusual: for one thing, my father had a job, not universal in those days, not even altogether common, and so we had an income. For another thing, I was the first child of a favorite daughter; yes, honestly; many hands sewed and crocheted for me, many fingers tucked and tatted. For me.

And I did feel my importance. Oh, my, yes.

You think I cannot remember this, but I can. Many children, maybe all of them, remember far more than they ever tell the grownups.

We were dancing in a circle, playing a child's game, Ring-Around-a-Rosy, popular then, maybe still. Well. Surely still.

I believe we might have been in a room in Aunt Anna's house, the house by the river. Aunt Anna was Paulie's mother and my godmother. I think the room may have been a dining room, or an alcove off a dining room; in any case there had to have been space enough for our circle.

* * *

One day last summer I was at a get-together of some of the women in the family: at my cousin Dolly's apartment. Dolly is old now and has had to give up her house in Robbinsdale: her sister Tildy was there, and Dolly's daughter Serene, whom I hardly recognized, she has gotten so gray, and Diana, Tildy's daughter-in-law, whom I don't recall ever having met before that day. Myrna, my cousin Billy's widow. Her daughter Alix. Etc., etc.

A whole room full of women.

We have met like this now and then ever since I can remember. It used to be my aunts and my mother and us, their daughters; but now all that older generation is gone and my generation is hanging on by its teeth.

We've filled our ranks with Serene's generation: Alix, Diana.

My own daughter will have nothing to do with these get-togethers.

Your family is totally weird, she says.

My family: hear that? Not hers.

Suddenly, connected to nothing, Tildy said: to me: Joan, do you remember when we were kids, all of us dancing in a circle around the table in Grandma's kitchen?

Why, the room seemed to tilt for a second.

Grandma's kitchen? Is that where it was, then? and around the table? it surely could have been.

Hey, Tildy, I said—I felt like I was taking a terrible chance,

THE BOOK OF SAINTS & MARTYRS

going way out on a limb here—would Paulie have been there?

Paulie? said Tildy. He could have been. Sure. He would have been—what?—five?

Six, I said.

Maybe six, she said. And you were just little.

Two years old, I said.

No, I think you were bigger than that, Joan. I remember your head poking up over the top of the table.

She said.

And your shoulders. You had on a white dress.

Going on three, anyway.

Okay, going on three. That'll work. . . .

It would have been just before he died, she said. If he was there.

He was there. I said.

I remember the wake, she said. My goodness, he looked so bad. His face was bitten by fish. The undertaker tried to fix it, but it looked strange.

Strange. . . .

Malone's Funeral Home, she said.

We always used Malone's.

By this time everybody was listening. My word, said Myrna, did they have an open casket? Why on earth would they do that?

I remember, I said. Aunt Anna insisted on it. Aunt Anna was half crazy with grief.

No half about it, said Tildy. Anna was crazy

I can't believe you remember it. She said. To me. You were so little.

I remember. I said.

* * *

I remember darkness: a dark day. Winter? Maybe. Well: it must have been winter. I figured this out years later.

I have spent my life on this quest.

I remember glass behind glass; and light sparkling off glass; and dark wood. A corner cupboard, they used to have them, do they still? Angular in shape, fitted into a corner, and shelved for treasures fronted with glass. And locked.

There would have been me and Paulie; Paulie's brothers, younger than he, Billy and Cyril, named for saints, and having "Joseph," all of them, as second names: Paul Joseph, William Joseph, Cyril Joseph: because their mother, my Aunt Anna, my godmother, was as they said then, "devoted to Saint Joseph." Yes, indeed, Joseph the Carpenter was her man; not my Uncle Luke, who was a barber.

There would have been in our circle also my three girl cousins, a little older than the rest of us: Catherine's daughters: Loretta Anne, Dorothy Catherine, and Mathilda Antoinette: Lollie, Dolly, and Tildy.

Probably there was no one else; my own brothers had—by my reckoning—not been born yet: the one next to me in age, Arden Jr., was, if I have figured this out right, in my mother's womb just at that time. So: seven of us: cousins. Circling and dancing and holding hands; chanting and singing and falling down in a heap of arms and legs:

Ring around a rosy...
A pocket full of posies...
Ashes, ashes...
We all fall down.

Paulie was across the circle from me. His white suit caught my eye and held it. The suit seemed almost to glow in the dark day. I looked down at my dress: white also. Why, I said to myself, that one over there is Paulie, and *this one is me.*

Suddenly I wore joy like a second dress. I felt haloed, clothed in light. To know that there was an "I"; to know that there was at the same time a "Paulie," an Other; was such an illumination that it must have been like the first time Helen Keller attached a word to a thing: *water:* and suddenly all the world became accessible to her: to me. That feels presumptuous, to dare to say that; to link myself with Helen: and yet, why not? Surely we are all linked? Surely all illumination comes from the same light?

I looked across the circle at Paulie, and I fell in love, for the first time, and fatally: forever.

* * *

I do remember, I said: to Tildy, at the gathering at Dolly's apartment.

You were so little, she said.

Yes: I was: so little.

* * *

There is another memory of Paulie—I am just now putting this bit into my picture, I have lived my whole life insisting that I had only the one memory but I see now that there is another. I never counted this other memory as amounting to much, but now I think I was wrong: I think it does count.

We had a game, my three boy cousins and I, that we played on Sundays sometimes when we were all together. This game was strictly forbidden by the grownups—or at least certainly would have been forbidden if they had had any notion of what we were up to.

This is how it went: we played our regular games—marbles, hopscotch, Captain-May-I?—out on the sidewalk: and we kept an eye out for cars although it wasn't like today when a steady stream of cars flows down any street.

Paulie invented the game. Paulie was always our leader. One day he saw a car coming and he suddenly began to scream at the car. (At the car; truly; not at the driver.)

Stop! he shouted.

Waving his arms.

Stop!

He ran along beside the car, screaming at it and waving his arms: like a toreador taunting a bull. Hey! You! Car! Come and get me! Hey! Stop!

The driver turned a stunned face toward us, but he did not stop.

Now, obviously this game had no point. And since it had no point, it became increasingly important to embroider it and surround it.

The next time we played the game, a car came along and my cousin Cyril turned his backside to it and farted at it.

Oh my God, was this rich, or what? We rolled on the sidewalk in spasms of laughter.

Well, of course Paulie had to top that. Of course he did. Another car came along, maybe ten minutes later. At the last second, Paulie darted into the path of the car and the car hit him. Not hard—cars did not go as fast in those days as they do now, nor were they the juggernauts that they are today. But hard enough to knock him down.

The driver stopped. We all stopped. For heaven's sake. So this is what the grownups were on about. So this is what they meant when they said: Stay Out Of The Street.

Well, the driver stood Paulie up and dusted him off. And he kept saying: to us: He ran right out in front of me! The kid ran right out in front of me!

Paulie stared at him. He stared around at all of us. He looked like someone who had seen another country.

Take him home, you kids. Tell his folks that it wasn't my fault. . . .

Said the driver.

So we took him home, just down the street, to his own house. Aunt Anna's house. Uncle Luke's house.

Walked in with him.

Paulie got hit by a car, Cyril said.

Nobody heard him.

Paulie got hit by a car, Cyril said, louder.

That time, Uncle Luke heard.

What's that? he said. What's that about Paulie? He held his hand up to shush the other grownups. Then we could all see how important our news was: that Uncle Luke, shy and quiet, would shush the grownups for it.

Shh. He said to them. Shh. Something has happened to Paulie.

And into the quiet: *Paulie?* said Aunt Anna. What happened?

Paulie didn't speak. He just kept looking into a far distance that only he could see.

Paulie got hit by a car, Cyril said. We all chimed in: Car. Hit. Driver. Fault.

Well, of course you know that all hell broke loose. Aunt Anna cried and yelled, and our grandmother felt Paulie all over and counted his arms and legs and pronounced him whole, not a bruise on him, not a bone broken, a miracle. . . .

Thank you, Saint Joseph!

That was Aunt Anna; at last it seemed that her devotion had paid off.

Did we tell you to stay out of the street? Did we tell you?

That was my father, dressed in his ice-cream suit and wearing his new straw hat that he wouldn't take off, even in the house.

Did we tell you?

Yes, we said.

Oh, they told us. Yes. We looked with new respect at Paulie, who had done what he was told not to.

* * *

Did I really see that? Is that a real memory? Or is that just something I was told about afterwards? It could be something I was told. And yet I seem to remember it—I seem to see it clearly. But could I have seen it? It would have to have been in the summer that I was two years old; careless as my parents were, would they have let me play unsupervised in the street at age two?

I seem to remember my father saying afterwards: meaning Paulie: *that child was doomed. I saw it in his face the day he got hit by the car. After that he wanted death. I saw it.*

Truly. My father was a strange, sweet man: who could say things like that.

* * *

Anna was the middle one of my grandmother's five daughters. Five girls and three boys. Surviving, that is; a boy, the baby William, Bernard's twin, and a girl, Josette, died in a diphtheria epidemic.

My mother—in a rare instance of self-revelation, mostly she kept her thoughts and memories to herself—told me once about that epidemic.

* * *

My mother never got sick. In all her life, in all the part of her life that I was with her, that I could watch this, I knew her to have maybe two little colds. And even they didn't amount to much. A little sniffling for two or three days and a cold was over.

She said it herself: I never get sick.

There was always some anger around it when she said it. It was as though "getting sick" was a privileged position that had been denied to her.

Oh, well, you know that I never get sick . . .

And: *I never got to stay home from school. The others got to stay home sometimes, but not me.*

Let me see your tongue, Elizabeth, my mother would say.

And: *Let me feel your forehead.*

And then: *You are not so sick, Elizabeth. You can go to school.*

My mother's eyes, blue like my Grandma's eyes—in fact, she was the one who looked like Grandma, and she was the favorite daughter—my mother's eyes would seem almost to well with tears for a second when she said it: I never got sick: but then the tears, the bare hint of tears, would vanish, and my mother would again be the cool, cool person that I knew.

And in fact, you know, I came to believe that she did not feel anything, that she had no feelings. Honestly—it was a perfectly logical deduction for a kid to make from the evidence.

The way William and Josette died was apparently typical of events in my mother's life.

Everybody in the family came down with diphtheria at the same time; everybody from Grandpa to the twin babies got it. Except my mother and my Grandma.

Can you see it?—the mother and the little girl working around the clock, days, nights, to keep the sick ones comfortable: well: to keep them *alive.*

There would have been ten sick and those two well.

No, wait, Mary was at the convent then, and Uncle Cyril was gone. So there would have been eight sick.

We moved all the beds that we could manage into the parlor downstairs, my mother told me. In her soft, cool voice. *We lined everybody up like in a hospital ward so we could take care of them easier.*

Doctor?

No, no doctor came. Well. My mother knew as much as any doctor knew in those days.

We did what we could to keep the fever down.

We did what we could to help them breathe.

We went from one to another and opened their mouths and scraped the awful white stuff out of their throats and sucked it away with a glass straw.

As much as we could.

Again and again.

My mother taught me how to do it. I don't want to, I said. You must, she said. Or they will die.

We gave them spoonfuls of her herb tea.

And broth. Whatever they could swallow. When they could swallow at all.

My Elizabeth . . . My good little nurse . . . my mother said.

But I got so tired.

And William died anyway. And Josette died.

Did she see them die? She must have seen them die. After a while, it might have seemed no great shakes. So later when it seemed to her that it was okay for a child to see anything, to hear anything, to be left out of nothing, might that not also have been for her a logical deduction?

I never got sick: I can hear the complaint in her voice now, many, many years later, when they are all eight of them dead of one thing and another, and my mother is dead too, my grandmother too, they are all gone, all, like it says in the Bible story, like grass, cut down.

One day I said to my Mama, when she was an old lady herself, and apropos of her then list of physical problems: At least you haven't got anything that you can die of. . . .

And she said: If I haven't got anything wrong with me that I can die of, how am I going to get out of here?

* * *

Anna was always odd one out; at any rate it sounds like that from the stories I have heard. And from my own observation; I took to Anna from the start, and Anna took to me.

You were the only one who was like me, she told me many years later: one day when she sat in a chair in the living room of the tiny house she lived in at the end with Cyril, who had never married, who stayed with Anna in quiet and apparently willing servitude.

Maybe Paulie would have been like me, Anna said.

If there had been a daughter, I imagine it would have been the daughter who stayed; but there was no daughter; and so Cyril stayed, a servant to Anna all his life.

Anna never forgave him for not being Paulie.

* * *

After Paulie died, Anna would talk and talk to my mother, and carry on like crazy.

Well, and crazy is what they said she was.

I heard her sometimes when they didn't think I was listening. I was that awful kind of kid who sneaks around and hides and stays quiet, so no one realizes that they exist, and everyone says things they shouldn't hear.

Why couldn't it have been Cyril who drowned? Anna would cry. Or Billy?

Shh, my mother would say. They'll hear. . . .

And they did hear, of course they did; children always hear.

I'd give God Billy and Cyril both, Anna said; if only He'd give back Paulie. . . .

I pray sometimes, she said. God, take Billy or Cyril, I pray. *Give back Paulie.* . . .

And: Oh, Paulie was my darling heart! How can I live without my darling heart?

Elizabeth, she would say: to my mother. You pray too. You ask Him for Paulie, you tell Him to take the others instead.

I can't do that, Anna, my mother said: shocked. You know I can't do that. . . .

* * *

My mother told me a story: that Anna had another suitor before she married Luke: young Lochinvar out of the west. He was not a Catholic. He was a perfectly nice person apart from that, and very good-looking, so my mother said, but *he was not a Catholic.*

So my grandfather—an old-world tyrant named Felix Ignatius, yes, honestly—put his foot down on Anna's heart, and declared that she could not marry her lovely boy.

I wonder what his name was.

Lochinvar?—but he never came to rescue Anna at the altar. No. No one did. No rescue occurred.

And Anna married Luke. Luke was declared by my grandfather to be a suitable match for his middle daughter.

I remember that Anna had a wind-up phonograph. She sat sometimes in the house by the river that Luke bought for her and played the phonograph: one song, over and over, and tears running down her face and splashing onto her hands.

Roses . . .
*I give you . . . ro-*zes . . .
And hope their *ten . . .* der blossom*ing . . .*
Why is Aunt Anna crying, Mama? I said.
Oh: she is thinking sad thoughts: my mother said.
Is she thinking of Paulie?
Maybe. Or maybe she is thinking of someone else that she wanted to marry once . . . she might be thinking of him. . . .
*. . . my heart disclo-*zes*. . .*

* * *

Uncle Luke was a barber. I wore my hair then in a short Dutch-boy cut, and every once in a while, maybe every six or eight weeks, Uncle Luke would sit me down in a straight-backed wooden kitchen chair and cut my hair.

I can still feel the cold sharp scissors slipping gently, barely touching the skin, over my forehead, under my bangs, shaping my skull.

Snip.
Snip.
Go the scissors.
He was so gentle, so good and kind, my Uncle Luke.
I loved him in the same quiet way that he probably loved me, that he probably loved all the children, all the cousins, his own children too.

Anna? Who knows what he felt for Anna? Love? Maybe. Sure.

He cut all our hair. Hairs, we said. We were German, and *hairs* was the German construction. *Das Haar*—one single hair; *die Haare*—many hairs.

I can remember his face: ordinary, brown eyes, a baffled look, tentative smile: *What has happened to me? Can these really be my children? Paulie is gone. They say this woman is my wife. She doesn't want any more children. She hates this house. She wants a house away from the river. I can't buy another house. There isn't enough money. . . .*

* * *

Depression Days. There was never enough money. A couple of years after Paulie died Uncle Luke stopped being a barber and took a job at Grant Battery instead; where he could make more money. After a while he and Anna and Cyril and Billy moved into another house. But it was too late, of course. The horse was out of the barn. Paulie could not come back. God never sent him back, in spite of Anna's prayers. God would not make the deal she asked for. Billy and Cyril both lived for quite a long time. Well, and Cyril is still alive. He still lives in the little house that was Anna's last house, and far, far from the river. He is a taxidermist: that interest began many years ago, when he and my two brothers were little boys and laid trap lines out by the pole yards in North Minneapolis. They say the basement of the little house is full of stuffed animals: otters, mink, muskrat. Fox. They say he kept the best ones for himself, to stuff, and sold the pelts of the others.

* * *

When Luke was an old man, he had a stroke and had to be put into a nursing home—this was a family disgrace, we did not put our old people into nursing homes, we took care of them at home—they say that the stroke turned Luke mean, and he (they say) cursed God and Anna and everybody else, cursed life, and I thought: Ah . . . then there is a kind of justice after all, a kind of compensation, a kind of balance. . . .

I can't take care of him at home, Anna wailed, an old lady then herself. He's too *mean!* He's too *big!* I *can't*. . . .

My Uncle Luke *was* a big man, I suppose she couldn't have him at home. But we all said: thought: Well, that's Anna. She never *was* like the rest of us, was she? She never did care that much about family, did she?

* * *

None of us ever had to pay for Uncle Luke's haircuts. Of course. That was part of what family was about.

I still love to get my hair cut. I still feel, in any hairdresser's fingers my Uncle Luke's fingers, my Uncle Luke's scissors, snipping, snipping, moving, faster than light, snip, snip, across my forehead: gentle, delicate, precise.

My personal belief is that Anna couldn't bear to touch him. She would have had to touch him a lot after he had the stroke, wouldn't she? If she had kept him at home.

But Cyril would have helped her. Cyril was Luke all over again. It could have been—what is that awful word they have now?—doable. It could have been doable.

* * *

The river was the Mississippi, the Father of Waters, as they call it here. It runs through, or past, Minneapolis and St. Paul, the Twin Cities—one city on each side of the river.

The Father of Waters, the mighty Mississippi, one of the greatest rivers in the world, certainly the greatest on the North American continent. It flows from a shallow, narrow—you can wade across it, and people do, I did, just to say they did; and step across it at its source, a little spring bubbling up from the earth—it flows from a shallow narrow beginning to its destination in the Gulf of Mexico, the Mississippi Delta at New Orleans. On its way, bisecting the country North to South, many rivers join it—the Minnesota, the Missouri—until from a modest stream it becomes a broad expanse of water, in some places a torrent. In Minneapolis it is wide, but a quiet, patient, waiting river. It has—it says—all the time in the world. In the early days, it provided the power for the great milling industries that rose up in the Twin Cities, and made them prosperous.

The house that Luke bought for Anna was near the river. The young couple acquired the house during the first years of the Great Depression of 1929, a time when a lot of homeowners had to sell out because they could no longer make their mortgage payments, or keep up with the taxes. The house by the river was sold to Luke and Anna for a song, I would be surprised if it cost more than two thousand dollars.

Anna's sister Catherine and her girls lived in a house in the same block: that was how Luke and Anna heard about the house that was up for sale and came to buy it when Anna was pregnant with Cyril. Catherine had only girls, and they were perfectly well-behaved Good Girls, and none of them ever disobeyed their parents' edict in the matter of the river: *Never go near the river, never, never.* But Anna began to worry about the river.

We can't stay in this house, she said.

We have to find another house.

To Luke.

Beleaguered, Luke said: quietly: I can't do it right now, Anna. We'll move to a different house as soon as I can afford it. . . .

You're such a worry-wart, Anna, said Catherine. Don't worry so much. *I* don't worry. . . .

You have girls, said Anna, as a series of boys popped out of her Catholic womb.

What difference does that make? said Catherine. Just tell them not to play by the river.

The river had a tremendous pull. I feel it even now; I have always felt it. My own daughter and I lived about a mile from the river years later and we often took lunches and played in the sand on its banks: built sandcastles and made sand castings, down where the showboat is anchored now, on the Washington Avenue side of the University of Minnesota East Bank campus.

I have walked across the covered bridge that joins the East Bank and the West Bank of the University, and have stood just in the middle and stared into the great flow and felt it wanting me.

Once, just at that spot, I consigned the body of a cat, killed I guess by a car, to the river, wrapped in a nice silk scarf and casketed in a shoe box. A black cat; I thought it was my own cat, Minnie, who had vanished, but Minnie turned up whole and healthy the next day, so it was someone else's cat that I gave to the river.

The river is part of the life of the Twin Cities: the cities' heart: you can't go far, or often, without seeing, or crossing, the great stream. Brown, muddy, enigmatic, not exactly a friendly river; an old, patient river, from the dawn of time.

* * *

Was Paulie Lochinvar's child? It is tempting to me to think so. Why not? It could have been, couldn't it? These things happen. Certainly Cyril and Billy looked like Luke, and Paulie looked like . . . well, not like Luke. Luke was of the earth. Paulie was from light.

* * *

One day: We are going to see Paulie.

I am so excited, I am skipping along with my hand in my father's hand and my mother is walking beside us carrying Arden Junior, who is just a new baby, only a few weeks old, maybe two months old.

I hate Arden Junior.

Be careful of your shoes, Joan, my mother says.

There is still snow on the ground, but it is dirty snow. Summer is far away, but the real winter is gone, melted.

I stop skipping and make my way carefully among puddles and mud-patches. I have on my white Mary Janes again. I have my white dress on too. Well, of course. We are going to see Paulie at last—of course I am all dressed up.

You'd better carry her, Arden, says my mother.

My mother's name is Elizabeth. Elizabeth is the name of a saint, and she is in *The Book of Saints and Martyrs* that Mama reads to me. Saint Elizabeth was important, like God's aunt or something.

Like Anna is my aunt. Like Catherine is my aunt. And Irma, and Sister Dominic in Tacoma, Washington.

My father is all dressed up too, in his ice-cream suit. He is wearing his new straw hat. My mother says that it is too early in the season to wear the hat, but my father says he doesn't care, he is going to wear it anyway, he likes his hat.

Dressed for a wedding, he says. And I'm going to a funeral.

He picks me up and carries me over the rest of the puddles. Oh, nice, I am not going to get my Mary Janes dirty, so Mama will not be mad at me. And I get to hug this big marvelous Daddy. I feel very, very safe, and very happy.

I love you, Daddy, I whisper into his ear, which is right near my mouth.

He hugs me tight against his scratchy ice-cream suit coat.

We walk up the sidewalk to a big house.

Is this where Paulie is now? I say.

This is not the house where Billy and Cyril and Paulie and Aunt Anna live. And Uncle Luke.

No answer. Daddy only squeezes me harder, too hard, and I squeak like my rubber toy. I am squeaking like my rubber toy, Daddy, I say. Into his ear. And then he squeezes me even harder. He is not smiling at all. We go up the cement steps to the big door at the top and the big door opens by itself, like magic, and there is a man standing behind it, and the man bends over to us a little bit. Everything is very quiet. It is like in a fairy tale, like the magic castle, where everything happens.

Paul Dannheim, says my father to the man.

That is Paulie's whole name, I know that. Paul Joseph Dannheim. We all have to know our whole names and our addresses, in case we get lost. My whole name is Joan Elizabeth Theresa Shepherd. I live at 4351 Sheridan Avenue North in Minneapolis, Minnesota.

I am named for my mother and my grandmother and a saint named Joanavark.

The man waves his hand, pointing at another door.

There, sir, he says to my Daddy. He calls my Daddy Sir. Madam. He says to my Mama.

My Daddy sets me down onto my Mary Janes on the carpet.

We have to be very quiet now, Dolly, he says. My father calls me Dolly. I don't know why. My real name is Joan. We have to remember that this is a funeral, he says.

What is a funeral, Daddy, I say.

I told you before, he says. Your Mama told you. A funeral is when somebody dies. Don't talk so loud, he says. You have to be quiet at a funeral.

But where is Paulie? I hold onto my Daddy's hand and look around. Why! Up there in the front is Aunt Anna, sitting on a chair, and there is Uncle Luke, sitting beside her. Luke, that was a big saint too, somebody who actually knew Jesus.

And there is Grandma.

There's Uncle Luke, I say. There's Aunt Anna. There's Grandma.

I try to pull away to go and talk to them, but my Daddy holds onto my hand and pulls me back.

Shh, he says.

Mama hands Arden to Daddy. Then she walks right up to the front of the room and puts her arms around Aunt Anna and says something to her.

Aunt Anna starts to cry, and then Mama starts crying too.

Why are they crying, Daddy? I say.

Damned if I know, says my Daddy.

And then: they must feel sad. He says.

But why.

Because Paulie is dead. Says my Daddy.

Where is Paulie? I say. When are we going to see Paulie?

My father hands Arden to one of my Aunts, maybe Aunt Catherine. Then he picks me up again and carries me up to the front.

There is a white thing like a pretty bed there, and Paulie—is that Paulie?—is lying in it. Is that Paulie? I say, and Shh, my Daddy says.

* * *

Why was Paulie just lying there? and why did he look so funny? He had his white suit on, that I remembered from the circle, and long brown stockings, and his hands were folded on his chest like when you pray, and there was a little white rosary twisted around his fingers, but his fingers looked so strange and his face looked strange too and the brown stockings looked like

big sausages

And: Why are Paulie's legs so fat? I said.

* * *

He had brown stockings on, I said to Tildy at the get-together of family women that I told you about before. Why did he have brown stockings on? Why not white?

I don't remember brown stockings, said Til. I think the casket was closed on the bottom. Like they always are.

He had brown stockings, I said. I remember.

***

Why are Paulie's legs so fat? I said.

Mama came. Shhh, she said. You'll make Aunt Anna feel bad. . . .

And apparently I did make Aunt Anna feel bad, because she let out a great loud yell and slid off her chair and lay on the floor there and she made awful noises and Uncle Luke got down beside her and tried to touch her and Aunt Anna was a kind of a fat lady and when she plopped on the floor she made a large squish sound and

She hit Uncle Luke's hands away

She started screaming. Paul! Paul! she screamed. I can't bear it, she screamed, and she cried and snot was coming out of her nose like when you have a bad cold and spit was coming out of her mouth and Try to control yourself Anna said Uncle Luke and

Let Anna grieve, said my Grandma. Let Anna be.

I still needed to know why Paulie's legs were so fat. I still needed to know.

***

This is barbaric, my father said, to my Grandma. Take the little one out, said Grandma. Why did you bring her here? She iss too little to be here. My father picked me up and carried me to the back of the room and out of the room and out onto the street. For Christ's sake, he said: to himself, it seemed like. She's just a baby, what did they expect her to do? Kneel and say a goddamn rosary?

Listen, Dolly, he said to me. Out of the depth of dark recent experience, let me give you some advice: never marry a Catholic. They are barbarians. . . .

I hung onto his neck. What's a barbar, what you said? I said.

And: Daddy, why were Paulie's legs so fat? Why did he look so funny?

I'm going to take you across the street, he said, and buy you an ice-cream cone. How would you like that?

Yes, but . . .

Daddy, why were . . .

I'll tell you after the ice-cream cone, he said. But he never did tell me. And I forgot about asking after a while and the ice-cream with Daddy was good, I didn't get to be with Daddy alone very much any more because there was a new baby now, a little boy to—what Daddy said—carry on the name, and I dripped ice-cream onto my shoes and my Daddy got down on the floor in the ice-cream store and wiped them clean with his handkerchief and then he got up and showed me how to eat an ice-cream cone so it wouldn't drip, licking it first around the edge close to the cone and only taking a bite out of the top when I had all the drips licked off.

* * *

I did get the answer eventually. Maybe thirty years later I asked again, my mother this time, and my mother said: Why, his legs were swollen from being in the water so long.

Of course.

And what was wrong with his hands.

What was wrong with his face.

His hands were nibbled by fish when he was in the river all that time.

Said my mother.

I thought he had mittens on. I thought it was winter.

I said.

I suppose his mittens came off, my mother said.

It seemed that the mittens had stayed tied around his neck attached to idiot-strings (they called them that, yes!—Do they still?) that kids wore under their coats in those days, up the arms and across the shoulders; but they came off his hands in the water.

His nose was bitten off too. Fish will do that, you know; they'll eat off anything that sticks out. My ex-husband (from whom I have been divorced now for more years than I was married to him) for example had a wart on his elbow and every time we went swimming the fish would swarm to him and try to get that wart. He finally had it removed, it was such an annoyance.

My mother said: The undertaker repaired his fingers with wax, but they didn't look right, did they?

No they didn't, I said.

His nose too, she said.

I'm surprised you remember any of it all that long time ago, said my mother.

I remember, I said.

You were so little, said my mother.

* * *

They held an open casket funeral because Anna insisted upon it. The undertaker and the priest tried to reason with her, they say, but how could they put it to her? The flesh is eaten off your child's bones, could they have said that? His nose is gone? No, of course not. The body is not in a suitable condition for review, that's what they would have said.

Don't say "body"! Anna would have screamed at them. *That's not a body, that's Paul!* I can hear it, absolutely. I knew her so well. I knew them all so well. They are all gone now. Mama and Daddy and Uncle Luke and Anna; even Billy; all dead themselves, so what does it matter?

Only to me. Only to that other child who still lives in me.

Maybe to Cyril, who lives alone now in the little house far from the river.

Maybe to Billy's children, Alix and Emma and Eloise. No saints' names there. We have wandered from our source.

Anna, they would have said, the body doesn't matter. It's the soul that matters.

I want Paul's body back! Anna would have cried. *God can keep his soul!*

Right, Anna. I'm with you. It was the body that I loved too and the little white suit and the perfect flesh and the hair and the dazzling, glowing face in the dark room.

I never forgave my mother, but I forgave Aunt Anna everything. Always.

* * *

I pieced together over many years the story of what had happened to Paulie, and when. It was for whatever reason important to me to know exactly when. Well, but it was important to me to know all that could be known. One piece my mother gave me—which was the only piece that in any way dated events—was that Arden Junior had been a newborn in her arms when she wandered up and down the river with Aunt Anna, both of them calling and calling for Paulie.

And Arden was born on February 1. So maybe Paulie drowned around the middle of February. Because they said he was in the water for six weeks, and they found him in March. So to say mid-February is cutting it fine.

* * *

My mother knew that calling to Paulie was hopeless—of course she did—but she did it anyway to placate Anna. Anna was entirely off her head. They say that she became really crazy during that six weeks when they couldn't find Paulie's body. A wild wail came into her voice then that never left it; all my life I heard that wail in her voice: the smallest things that she talked about, the most ordinary things, a walk around the block, the price of celery, a talk with a neighbor, became subjects for dirges.

You would have thought she was Cassandra calling out doom when she told about baking a pie.

* * *

So there they go, the two sisters, wandering up and down the river bank, the Mississippi, the Father of Waters, one of the sisters carrying a tiny new baby, the other mad with grief that her firstborn has been torn from her arms by this terrible river; calling and calling, the two of them.

Pauleee! Pau-au-au-leee! I can hear them, see their feet slipping and sliding in the wet-leaf-strewn melted-snow earth of February, of March.

Paulie!

My mother knows this is insane, of course she does. But she calls out because it eases Anna for her to do so.

He's alive, says Anna. I know he's alive. I feel it. . . .

My mother cleaves to reason, all her life. But where would he be, Anna, if he were alive?

Don't say that! Anna screams. *Don't say that! Don't ever say that!*

So they trudge and call and the baby in Elizabeth's arms grows heavier and heavier.

Here, let me take the baby, says Anna.

But Elizabeth won't surrender Arden. She is—she tells me this many years later—afraid of Anna.

She thinks Anna is so crazy that she would throw the new baby into the freezing water to be with the other one. So Elizabeth holds onto her own child, carries him up and down the river bank for hours, while Anna calls for Paulie.

* * *

I don't think Anna ever really got over it, said Myrna, Billy's widow, that day at the ladies' get-together. I think she always mourned for Paulie. She always wanted to talk about it. And she'd cry and cry.

She never talked about it to me, I said. Never.

I wonder why?

Maybe she thought you were too little, said Myrna. Maybe she thought you wouldn't remember.

Maybe, I said.

Did Billy talk about it, I said.

No, said Alix. My Dad never wanted to talk about it.

I guess I'm not surprised: I heard Anna's voice from long ago: wailing: You pray Elizabeth. You pray that God will take Billy and Cyril, and send Paulie back. . . .

Jesus. Jesus.

* * *

Where am I, the little girl that was me, while all this goes on, this wandering on the river bank? And where are Billy and Cyril? Why, we are probably at Grandma's house, where Grandma lives with her youngest daughter, our Aunt Irma.

How can an aunt be a daughter? I puzzle about this. I am a daughter. But I am not an aunt.

I ask Grandma about this, but Grandma can't explain it. She tries, but I don't understand. Grandma doesn't talk very well. Grandma is from Germany, which is The Old Country. This is The New Country. Grandma came across the water on a boat. The ocean is a very large body of water. My Daddy told me that.

What is an ocean, Daddy.

An ocean is a very large body of water, Dolly. He says.

Body. Body of water.

But what I really meant to tell you here is that Grandma doesn't talk very well. They spoke another language in The Old Country, which is German.

The language in this new country is English. Our Grandma doesn't speak English even as well as I do. She does it a little better than Billy but Billy is a baby. Not as small as Arden Junior, but still a baby.

But Grandma does not have to talk. Her face is old. She smiles a lot. Her eyes are blue. Her hands are kind. Wherever

Grandma is, is peace, love, safety. Wherever Grandma is, is home.

* * *

When I was eight or nine, I had pneumonia. I actually had to be in a hospital, a notable and rare eventuality in those days. While I was in the hospital, my fever ran so high that a lot of my hair fell out, and what was left was allowed to become a tangled, matted mass. It probably wasn't the fault of the hospital nurses—nuns, all, at St. Mary's, the city's Catholic hospital—no, remembering what I was like as a child, I probably bit them when they came near me with a comb.

When I got home, my mother sat me in a chair in the living room and tried to comb through the mess. I begged her to stop, I cried, but she persevered.

I don't think pain impressed my mother.

But my grandmother happened to be at our house that day.

Stop this, Elizabeth, she said to my mother.

But Ma! I have to get the snarls out!

Nein, she said. She took out of her big black pocketbook a little pair of scissors and she cut every mat and snarl from my hair, freeing some hairs and snipping others, carefully, carefully; it took a very long time.

Finally: There, she said. Now you can comb.

To my mother.

But it's all uneven, my mother said.

Ja, said my Grandma. But it will grow again.

You do not understand pain, Elizabeth, she said. I wonder how can that be?

* * *

I can see my grandmother in my mind's eye now. I am an old lady now myself—these things happen, dear, wait and see—and I still see her holding Billy on her lap in the kitchen of the old house on Second Street, I see her holding a turning fork in her hand and turning over *fatigman* in the old black cast-iron frying pan.

I see her in the garden in the summertime, digging around the roots of the marigolds that grew under the wooden back stairs and round the outhouse.

Why do you dig around the roots, Grandma?

Ach, child, I haff to give them some air, *die Blumen*—the flowers, they need air, chust like you, Johanna. . . .

Johanna. She called me Johanna. Yo-hanna.

That is German for Joan. My name: Joan.

Which is feminine for John. *John:* from the Hebrew: *God is gracious.*

You can't get much better than that. For a girl's name.

* * *

I breathe air in and out through my nose for a long time, feeling the air go in and out, feeling me needing the air.

Then I try not to breathe in any air, to see if I really do need it.

Good Heavens, Johanna, you are turning blue! my Grandma says. Breathe, child. Breathe.

I *do* need air, Grandma, I say when I can speak.

My Grandma looks worried and she watches me to see that I keep breathing.

* * *

Paulie walked on the ice of the river in February that year, on what I later learned to call "rubber ice."

"Walking on water," I say to myself whenever I think of it and I think of it often, probably every day, and I know that this phrase is totally inappropriate, bordering on blasphemy, and imputing Christ-like notions to Paulie; but he *was* my little white Christ, don't you see? so shining he was. . . .

And if he had worn brown that day in the circle, say, or

green, would the memory be as sharp? Would it find its home in my heart like a white knife? Who can say? Who ever knows things like that? Life turns on such small occasions. I think of Kurt Vonnegut's beer can opener, and I shout: Yes! Yes! *that's the way it is!*

So Paulie walked on rubber ice, with his friends; they were all of course absolutely forbidden to try the ice, and as a matter of fact the river itself was forbidden to all of them.

Don't go by the river, Paulie. Danny. Roger. John.

Stay away from the river. . . .

* * *

For a while the other little boys—Danny, Roger, John—were afraid to come and tell what had happened. But finally one of them came to the house and told Anna that he had seen the ice break, he had seen Paulie slip under the ice.

* * *

When my own child died, about twenty-five years later, I chose not to have a public viewing. The only people who saw him before he was buried were his father and a friend. I couldn't go even for the funeral—I was too sick.

Aunt Anna talked about it for months, she wouldn't leave it alone.

Oh, Joan, she cried. Wailed, in that banshee wail of hers. Oh, why didn't you let anyone see your baby? Oh, why?

I did not want it, I said.

Oh, she cried, oh, I would have *loved* to see your baby, Joan! I would have *loved* to see him!

* * *

We were going to see Paulie.

I was so excited; that last time we saw him had been: when he was lying in that pretty bed and wouldn't get up, wouldn't get up: unsatisfactory.

This would be better.

Bound to be.

Grandma went out into the wonderful sunny day, big sun was jumping off the little yellow suns of the marigolds under the stairs

sun

Grandma

marigolds

oh wonderful day we are going to see Paulie.

My Grandma kneels down by the marigolds she has her blue apron on and she is careful to kneel only on grass not in the dirt she has a digger which she sticks in the dirt around one of the marigolds.

What's that Grandma? *this is a trowel, child.* what are you doing Grandma? *oh, I am digging up this flower, Johanna.* why, Grandma? *oh, we are going to take this flower to Paulie . . .*

She marks a circle with the trowel around the chosen flower.

She pushes the trowel down deep along the circle marks, and then she pushes on the trowel backwards so that the flower comes up with its own bit of dirt around its roots.

Why are you doing it like that, Grandma?

Like what, Johanna?

Why don't you just pull it out like I pulled the onions out?

This flower is not like an onion, Johanna, an onion is to eat, but this flower we are going to plant again so that it will grow in a different place . . .

I must dig it up very carefully so that I do not damage the roots. She says. If the roots are too much damaged, the plant will not grow in the new place, it will not survive.

Not survive, not survive, not survive.

What is not survive. Grandma?

Not to live, Johanna, not to be alive.

Live.

Alive.

* * *

My Daddy has his straw hat on and he is wearing his ice-cream suit. I love his ice-cream suit. He says it is called an ice-cream suit because it is the color of cream and it has little red and green flecks in it like that nice kind of chocolate chip ice-cream and I say, But Daddy chocolate chip ice-cream has *brown* spots, and he says, red, green, brown, what's the difference, a spot is a spot, use your imagination Dolly, are you going to be like your Mama, with no imagination?

My Grandma says I have a very big imagination, I say.

Yes, well, says Daddy.

If your Grandma says it, it must be true.

My Daddy likes my Grandma a lot, I know that.

Your Grandma is a very great lady, he says. If your Grandma says something is true then it *is* true.

* * *

My Daddy takes his hat off and lays it on the kitchen table.

Is that an ice-cream hat, Daddy? I say.

You could say so, he says. You could call it that.

Can I have it Daddy?

You can not have it, he says. You can touch it and you can try it on, but you can not have it. That hat is mine.

He goes out of the kitchen. The screen door swishes shut behind him with a little bang.

My Hat.

I think about it.

That hat is Daddy's.

The marigold is Grandma's marigold, and she is going to give it to Paulie.

This is something like the onions.

I pulled up the onions and they were Mrs. Erickson's onions and I didn't know they were hers, I thought if they were growing in the ground they could belong to anybody, and I pulled them up oh beautiful the shiny white balls and the lovely green sticks and the nice dirt and Mrs. Erickson was very mad at me she came over and yelled at my Mama and my Grandma was there too. You have to teach this child some respect for private property, she yelled.

And my Grandma said She iss chust a baby, she did not know. . . .

* * *

The hat was on the kitchen table and I picked it up and tried it on my head.

It was too big, it flopped around. It was a flat round hat with a flat piece sticking out all around it. Stripes of what look like braids, like my Aunt Anna braids her hair, like my Mama braids dandelions for us, were stuck together in a hat shape, around and around.

How did they do that?

There was a little thread sticking out at the edge where the stripe finished.

I pulled at the thread a little bit.

It pulled loose in a wonderful zig-zag of white thread.

Oh!

I pulled some more.

More zig-zag.

More and more.

Suddenly the thread came loose, I had the end of it.

But.

Oh gosh. Oh horror. The hat was gone.

This might be worse than the onions.

I understood everything suddenly. Everything.

Without the thread there could be no hat.

This was an important thing! A wonderful thing to know! But I was pretty sure that my Daddy would not understand this.

I was pretty sure that he would only understand that he did not have his hat anymore. I tried to put the braid of straw back into a hat shape and I was doing fairly well with it, the straw looked sort of like a hat again, and then Grandma and Mama and Daddy came into the kitchen, and Mama was carrying the new baby who was not so very new any more but who was named after Daddy, Arden Quarles Junior.

There was a third name too, a saint's name, but nobody even remembered what that was after a while.

I hated that baby and I wanted his name and I knew that my own name was not good enough.

And Grandma was carrying the flower which was now in a little pot.

We're off! said my Daddy.

Where is my hat here it is he picked up the hat-shape and it fell apart into loops and loops of straw braid.

What the *hell!*

He yelled.

And then at me: What Have You Done To My Hat?!!

I was so scared, I saw that he really cared about that hat, but I didn't mean it, I didn't mean to do it, I didn't mean to make it fall apart, I just pulled the little thread with its little zig-zag points, one this way, one that way . . .

My mother seemed to be holding her breath.

But:

Ach, said my Grandma. She didn't mean to do it, Arden. She iss little, she iss chust a baby. . . .

She's not too little to learn about private property, my father said softly. Whispered. Apparently this was too awful to even yell about.

Private property.

I knew private property

I learned *that* with the onions.

This wasn't about private property, this was about pulling on a little thread, and how the thread made the hat stay together, and how the hat was not a hat without the thread. . . .

Yes, well, said my Grandma: not today. She will not learn private property today. This iss Memorial Day and we go to take this flower to remember Paul. . . .

Can I carry the flower, Grandma? I said.

No, Johanna, she said. You are too little to carry the flower.

You can carry the water, she said.

She took a glass jar out of the cupboard and filled it from a pail of water near the sink. She used a tin dipper and poured the water into the jar with the dipper and she gave me a drink from the dipper.

And when I stop and live in my tongue for a moment I can taste that water still, clean, sharp, cold, tasting of the earth, where it came from, the pump and the well under the stairs, and of the tin dipper.

Here, she said, you can carry this, and she put a cover on the jar of water and put the jar into my hands.

Iss this too heavy, Johanna? she said.

No, Grandma, I said: It's just right. . . .

Just Right . . . the porridge in the story of The Three Bears was *Just Right.* . . .

My Daddy picked up the straw loops of his hat and threw them into the iron cook stove, the part where they lit the fire when Grandma cooked. Might as well get some good out of it, he said.

We all got in the car, which was a Model A Ford, I still have an old photo of that car, my mother is standing in front of it on her wedding day, holding her wedding bouquet.

We get into the car and Grandma and I sit in the back seat and she is holding the flower and I am holding the jar of water and in the front seat my mother is holding Arden Junior who has not yet begun to be called Sonny and my father has no hat on and I am very sorry I spoiled the hat I am very sorry

Daddy I'm sorry, I say

Don't mention it, he says

Done is done, he says

but I am carrying the water and I am terribly proud to be doing that I am terribly proud that I am not too little to carry it and I hold it very very carefully so I don't drop it and so it doesn't spill and doesn't leak

What is the water for, Grandma? I say

The water iss for the flower, Johanna, my Grandma says. We will pour the water on the roots of the flower when we plant it, she says.

The flower cannot live without water.

She says.

Air and water. Yes. Okay.

An important thing then; carrying the water.

* * *

The car stops at the edge of a little road that does not go straight like the road by our house or by Grandma's house, but turns and curves quite pleasantly

it is more like the roads out in the country, which is where my Daddy takes us in the car sometimes on Sundays after church, but this is not the country this place is right in the city and it has a big fence around it and we drive past a gate made of big stones and I think this is beautiful the stone gate and the fence and the green grass and many little trees and some big trees and there are statues all around I know what statues are. Grandma has a statue of Mary, who is God's mother, in the garden in the back yard by her house

and the curving road is beautiful, and the blue, blue sky, I know that the sky is where God lives and I feel God very close today I could talk to him like I do sometimes if I have time but I don't have time I am carrying the water and that takes all the time

and we all get out of the car and we walk and I carry the water quite carefully only once I forget and I skip once *I am going to see Paulie!* and, Do Not Skip, Johanna, my Grandma says, only not meanly, just saying it. Do not the water spill, she says and I stop skipping and I walk along quite quietly carrying the water in the glass jar and Mama carries Arden Junior and Grandma carries the yellow flower and my Daddy carries nothing he just walks along with us and I know he is still mad about his hat I wonder if he will stay mad all day and we don't walk very far only a little way if I looked back I could still see the car quite near and then we come to a place where there is a little hill, sort of a hill, a little *tiny* hill, like I could make with the sand by the alley at home, not a hill like God makes and

Here we are, says Grandma.

I don't understand. Where? Where are we? And if we are *here,* then where is Paulie?

My Grandma kneels down and this time she does not have her blue apron on and she doesn't seem to care if she gets her dress dirty and she starts to dig a hole in the little hill. She has brought the trowel along—why! I didn't know she brought that, where was it, in her pocketbook?—and she cuts the grass out very carefully in a round circle and she lifts the grass away and sets it on the side and nobody says anything and a cloud comes over the sun and it is cold for a second and then the cloud is gone and it is warm again.

She digs the dirt out of the hole and she makes a pile of it on one side and then she tips the flower out of its pot and she sticks the flower with its own dirt around the roots, she sticks it in the hole.

I am simply fascinated, I love this planting business, I want to learn how to do this, I want to do the things that my

Grandma does, and I want to be like Grandma and so I watch her very carefully.

She pats the earth down around the flower and it sits there just fine and it seems as though it will be all right in its new place and the sun shines on its little flower face and its face is like the big sun, a little sun, and

You can put the water now, Johanna, my Grandma says.

Pour it right around the roots.

She says.

* * *

I do what Grandma says to do. I kneel down and bend over the little hill, like Grandma did, down quite close to the flower, and I take the cover off the jar and lay it down on the grass and then I begin to pour the water right down onto the roots of the flower and the flower is like a bright yellow sun and I can see that there will be more suns, the flower has many more buds on it that can open up, if the flower *survives,* and the water pours with a wet, gurgling, pouring sound out of the glass jar and it pours and pours and

the water

goes

down

soaks

into the earth

and down

past the roots of the flower

and down

and down

and suddenly I know something.

The sun turns dark. The flower shrivels. The sky closes up and becomes a blue cloth that comes down very close and suffocates me so that I have no air to breathe.

Paulie is under there, I say.

* * *

Flashes: of memory.
Didn't you tell her about death, Elizabeth? my Grandma says.
Well of course I did, my mother says.

* * *

My mother lies.

* * *

I get the door of the car open I slam myself into the back seat, I try with my fingernails to claw my way through the leather, I want to *go into it,* I want to *go through it,* I want to
disappear
and I am screaming and screaming and I think everyone can hear me screaming except me I can hear nothing there is no sound at all but I can feel my mouth being open
a hole
a hole with no tongue in it
This is what death is then, death is being under the dirt, death is breathing dirt and not breathing air, there is no air to breathe under the dirt, will I be dead then too? Death is breathing water.
I will never see Paulie again and the dirt will cover me too the dirt covers me I lie with Paulie in the pretty bed under the dirt and my Grandma digs a hole for me and plants a flower and I pour the water and the water runs down into my eyes
into Paulie's eyes
the water runs down into the earth and runs down and
the marigolds
under the stairs
under the earth
all the people. All.

* * *

Ashes. Ashes. We all.

***

They took me over to Aunt Catherine's house the night that Arden Junior was born.

February 1 it was—I know that now. Or maybe January 31, if he was born in the morning. Because I remember very clearly that it was night when I went to Aunt Catherine's.

Aunt Catherine's house—I see suddenly that I do not think of it also as Uncle Gabriel's house. I believe that is because the men seemed to count for very little in our family.

The women were everything.

They were all terrifically strong: Catherine and Anna and Grandma and Irma and Mary, who became Sister Dominic. My mother? Well, yes, in her different way; my mother too.

The men were just sort of *there*—the purpose of men was to provide a living for women and children. It did not matter very much what sort of *people* the men were; as long as they were "good providers."

Uncle Luke was a "good provider"—I knew that, I heard my aunts talking.

Uncle Gabriel was not such a good provider.

But good provider or not, it didn't matter much what kind of people they were.

My Daddy? Well. He was in a way the exception. It mattered to everybody what kind of person *he* was. To this day, my cousin Tildy says, Your dad was wonderful, a party was not a party without your dad.

But even he got drawn into the provider role. Even he, I think, took some of his sense of importance—and he did feel important, oh, yes, just as I do—from the fact that a woman had married him and that he was fathering children.

And our family lived in a house that we *owned*. It was truly Our House. It was not rented from somebody else.

Catherine and Gabriel and the girls: Dolly and Lollie and

Tildy: lived in a rented house. I didn't know much, but I knew that. So: they took me to a rented house that I didn't visit very often, and that I didn't want to go to on this night, and they told me that I had to stay there—alone!—with people I didn't like very much, *because my mother was going to the hospital to have a baby.* . . .

Where was my Mama? What was happening to her?

I find myself wondering now, as I write this, why they didn't take me to Aunt Anna's house where I knew everyone and was perfectly comfortable; and in a sudden flash I understand that this birth had to have occurred right around the time that Paulie died.

It could have been that the whole rest of the family—Grandma and Irma and everyone—was rallied around Aunt Anna because of this death, and that was why I had to go to Catherine's house.

And that—I imagine—might also have been the reason I was so terribly frightened that night. The whole family would have been frightened, they would all have been in a state of shock—and then, into the maelstrom, my mother's second child was born.

* * *

They tell me I am going to have a little brother or sister when I wake in the morning. Why would anyone suppose that that idea would comfort me in any way?

Why would I want such a thing? In the first place, what *was* it? I was not entirely sure; except that it must be another person; and in the second place I had my cousins, I didn't need more people; if a little brother or sister was *people,* I didn't need any more, and I didn't want any more.

* * *

My cousin Dolly had "heart trouble." "Heart trouble" was a disease and diseases were something you caught from other people. You got diseases from being near people who had diseases. And "heart trouble" was a very bad disease, I knew this because my Mama and Grandma talked about it sometimes and Grandma said how she prays for Dolly, and how she is afraid that Catherine and Gabriel "won't raise" Dolly. I don't know what that is, "won't raise," but I am sure it is bad, and I don't want to sleep in the same bed with Dolly because when I wake up in the morning I will have "heart trouble" and also a new brother or sister and they "won't raise" me, oh, no, they "won't raise" me....

Eventually, of course, being smaller than these others, I am overpowered and put to bed beside Dolly; also—eventually—I fall asleep. When I wake up, I do not have "heart trouble"— (What do you mean, you *haff* caught heart trouble? says my Grandma later: little Johanna? You don't *catch* heart trouble, you just *haff* it....) but I do have a baby brother.

I hate Arden until we are both adults. I hate Dolly even longer than that: only in the last ten or fifteen years have I seen that she is basically a fairly decent human being, doing the best she can, a little silly, a person given to uttering really dumb and devastating insults, with her big silly brown eyes wide— "For heavens sakes, I sure didn't mean anything by that"—but, like most of the rest of us, fundamentally a pretty good person who means well most of the time.

And they did after all "raise" her. Since she is still with us, probably about seventy-five years old by now, and as far as I know okay apart from sciatica—which isn't catching either— they must, you will agree, have "raised" her.

* * *

Myrna, Billy's widow—Billy died about fifteen years ago of a pulmonary embolism, on New Year's Day, just two days after he received a clean bill of health from a doctor in his yearly physical; make what you will of that; I know what I think—Myrna said to me: You know, Alix has all the newspaper clippings from the time when Paulie drowned. There's even a picture of Anna down by the river, calling to Paulie.

I thought my heart would stop.

Can I—can I see them? I said. Sometime? Not really wanting to. But yes, wanting to.

Ambivalence, they call what I have.

Not right away or anything, I said. But sometime.

Sure, said Myrna. I'll call you. We'll get together.

* * *

When my Aunt Anna hobbled toward the end of her life, there did after all come a time when the doctor said she had to go into a nursing home. That happened because she had one day been trying to clean out a furnace grate in the floor of the little house she shared with Cyril, and she fell into the open grate and stuck there up to her armpits for many hours, until Cyril came home from his car-wash job and found her and got her out: banged up and bruised and black-and-blue practically all over.

Poor Cyril. He didn't want to let Anna go to the nursing home. What would he do with his life? then? But the doctor insisted. Good God, man, he said: she has diabetes, heart trouble, ulcers on her legs, she's half blind and half deaf and she's wandering in her wits.

She can't be alone any more. I won't take the responsibility. Blah blah blah.

I went out to visit her in the nursing home in Robbinsdale where they put her: not often enough, but sometimes. My visits to her, I mean, did not occur often enough. Well. I hated to see her there, that was it. But I went anyway; sometimes with my mother and sometimes alone.

I took a friend along once when I went with my mother. Afterward: Your mother is jealous, the friend said. Of you and Anna.

No way, I said. My mother doesn't care enough about either one of us to be jealous.

Trust me, said my friend.

Once I went alone to see Anna and when I got there she was asleep. I didn't know whether to wake her or not. I sat quietly in a chair, not knowing, uncomfortable, and after a while she woke up, and moved on the bed restlessly, angrily, and said: Is someone here?

I'm here, Anna, I said: Joan.

Joan, she said. Come here where I can see you.

I came over to the bed and bent closer to her and took her hand.

I can't see you, she said.

I'll put your glasses on, I said, and did so: thick cataract lenses, this was long before lens implants were common. Settled the ugly black plastic frames on her nose, placed the bows properly on her ears.

Joan! she cried. In that clarion wail. How did it happen that she kept that young voice still in that old, old body?

Yes, it's me, I said.

Give me a kiss, she said. Reaching up her fat arms, flesh hanging off them as old women's flesh does.

I kissed her soft old cheek.

I always liked you, Joan, she said: cried. Sometimes I pretended you were my own little girl.

I know, Aunt Anna, I said. I always knew that.

You were like me, she said.

You were the one who taught me to sew, Aunt Anna, I said. When I was twelve. Do you remember?

I remember, she said.

I remember sewing a white dress for you when you were a little tiny girl.

She said.

I'm having an awful time here, Joan, she said. With my life. I wish God would take me. I pray to Him all the time to take me.

He will, I said. Soon.

He won't, she said.

Do you know why? she said. Squawked.

No, I said. Why?

I offered St. Joseph my death, she said.

This is a Catholic thing, in case you don't know. In case you are wondering. You offer your sufferings, whatever they may be, to atone for the sufferings of Christ.

Maybe they don't do that any more, but they did in the old days.

I told St. Joseph—said Anna—that whatever death God had in mind for me, I would accept it.

She held my hand tight in the vise-grip of age.

I made a mistake, she said.

I wish I hadn't done it.

Take it back, I said.

I can't, she said. They don't let you take it back.

* * *

Once, when Anna was still living at home, in the little house where Cyril lives still, far from the river, we—all the women—met there for the get-together. There was me and Myrna and Tildy and Lollie and Dolly (who was home on a vacation, something like that, she was married at the time and lived in Milwaukee), and my mother, Elizabeth. Six of us, and Anna. Well. That was enough. That was respectable. A quorum. So to speak.

Cyril was there too; in fact, Cyril had made the lunch and was for that day an honorary woman. Almost as good as a woman.

Tildy—may God help us all—had (I think out of boredom and dissatisfaction with her life; and why not?) Tildy had just become a charismatic Christian. Otherwise known as a Born-Again. Catholic, still, I think, but Born-Again.

She was in the stage where she was trying to convert everybody. Me.

Joan, do you know Jesus? she asked me once over lunch. Oh, I think so, Til, I said. No, Joan, I mean, Are You Saved By The Blood Of The Lamb?

Well, enough.

Look, Tildy, I said. You know I love you dearly, like you were my sister that I never had. But I would like to respectfully request that you just shut up about this stuff. If you don't, I won't meet you for lunch any more.

And I have to give Til credit: she did shut up.

That day at Anna's house, though, she said: Let's pray for Anna.

Let's pray for Anna to be healed.

(I already told you the list of things that were wrong with Anna: diabetes, deafness, blindness, ulcers on her legs, congestive heart failure, etc., etc. I never knew anybody else with more things wrong with them. The doc certainly had a point when he insisted that she go into a nursing home.)

(If Til could have managed it, it would have been a really spectacular healing.)

Do you want us to pray for you, Anna? I said.

Oh, sure, she said, reaching her hand out to me.

I took it, held it.

Tildy got on her other side and took Anna's other hand.

Then everybody joined hands, my mother holding my hand, then Lollie, then Dolly, then Cyril, looking sort of sheepish, etc., etc.

Until we made a circle.

Ring around a rosy: I thought.

Til talked. Prayed.

THE BOOK OF SAINTS & MARTYRS 163

Dear Lord. She said. Please look with mercy on your servant, Anna; etc., etc. On and on. A sing-song drone.

As Til prayed, Anna's face grew more and more peaceful. Happier and happier. Beatific, you could say. A goofy fat smile broke that dear old face pretty much from ear to ear.

When it was over: Oh, Anna said. Oh, that was almost as good as dying!

When I do die, she said, this is how I want it to be! with all my family gathered around me . . . and holding my hands. . . .

Afterwards, on the way home, my mother said to me: Do you think Tildy can heal people?

I think healings can happen, I said. I think miracles can happen. But do I think Tildy can do them?

No, I said. I don't.

I don't either, said my mother.

And when the time came, in the nursing home, Anna died alone.

* * *

In my dining room, resting on my mother's old cedar chest, I now have the box full of newspaper clippings and other stuff from the time Paulie died; Myrna brought it over about a month ago.

I've looked at it all a couple of times: read the clippings, touched the things Anna saved for so many years.

Like Myrna said, there is a news photo of Anna standing by the river: not fat at all as I remember her, but slim and elegant, looking lovely and tragic in a fashionable cloche hat and a beautifully cut knee-length coat, with those tiny-heeled pointy-toed shoes that they wore in the twenties and thirties.

I think I am shocked to see her so carefully dressed.

What did I want her to wear? Sack-cloth and ashes? Yes, maybe.

And wouldn't *I* try to look as good as I could if I knew I was getting my picture in the paper? No matter what was happening? Absolutely. I would.

* * *

There's other stuff in the box too. Letters from my Aunt Sister Dominic, Sister Mary Dominic, O.S.B., which is Order of Saint Benedict, about how all the nuns in the convent and all the children in the grade school in Tacoma, Washington, where my aunt was a teacher, were praying for Paulie to be found; then, after all hope was lost, by everybody except Anna, for Paulie's body to be found.

There's a stiff pair of leather mittens; I imagine they are the ones he wore the day he was drowned. Why else would she keep them in the box? There are no idiot-strings on them.

There's a lock of curly blond hair. Did she cut it off his head after he was found? I don't know.

There's dark brown hair woven and braided and tied into a Victorian mourning corsage: did Anna cut her hair when Paulie drowned and have it made into this? Who can know? now?

Who can ever know?

What *is* certain is that Paulie died; and Anna lived and I lived; after a fashion, both of us. Both of us living strange, rich, twisted lives, curled as we were around a drowned child's finger: nibbled by fishes, mended with wax.

* * *

I think: How do we do it? How do we ever manage it at all? All of us; how do we survive? How do we live from day to day on this hard planet—too hot, too cold, too dangerous?

The box—a Buster Brown box, do you remember Buster Brown, the little boy in the ads, with long curls and a starched white Peter Pan collar?—the box sits on my mother's cedar chest—Hope Chests, weren't they called?—that I have in my house now: uncomfortable, like an urn on the mantelpiece full of an uncle's ashes. I had thought that when I touched that box, read those clippings, held those mittens, the sky would fall. Again. But it didn't; I am trying to be honest here. The sky didn't fall. Nothing happened at all. I felt nothing at all. The important thing was the memory: unassailable in my mind; not the facts, and not the artifacts.

One of these days I'll have to give the box back to Myrna; well, really to Alix, to Billy's daughter, who seems to value it. Hey. Anna was her grandmother, and dearly loved from all I can make out. Of course she values it.

* * *

Myrna tells me that when her girls were babies, Anna would keep a drawer in the kitchen full of relatively harmless objects, and when the ladies came over for a get-together Anna would seat them around the kitchen table, take out the drawer, place it in the middle of the table, and plunk the current baby into the drawer. The baby—old enough to sit up, I guess—would be entertained by the drawer's contents for hours, and all the ladies could watch the baby and eat and chat at the same time.

My gosh, I said to Myrna. That's absolutely brilliant . . . Yes, wasn't it? said Myrna.

I adored Anna, she said. So did the kids.

Myrna was a kind of an odd-man-out too; or at least was different from most of the family; I took to her the first time I met her; when she was nineteen years old and Billy brought her to my parents' twenty-fifth wedding anniversary party. Forty-five years ago now. Forty-five or so.

* * *

Alix has two little daughters, Kim, who is nine, and Pammy, who is seven.

Pammy hasn't spoken except to her mother and her sister for four years. She has what they call "selective mutism." She doesn't speak in school or on the school bus; or to anyone else, not even to her grandmother, Myrna, who cries when she talks about Pammy.

Four years ago, Pammy's daddy left his wife and his daughters: just up and left them, not a word, never a word since.

And something else strange happened at just that time.

Do you remember the news stories about the house in New Brighton, which is a suburb in the first ring of suburbs around Minneapolis? where the police figured out that there were at least two murdered bodies buried in the yard and they dug and they dug all winter, all over the yard, a big yard, a double lot, great for children, dug it up, breaking the frozen earth with jackhammers? You remember that, the news was full of it for weeks. It was about four years ago.

Finally they did find the bodies, frozen in the winter earth; and dug them up. With jackhammers.

Well, that was Alix's house.

And Pammy stopped talking.

* * *

My life has always felt fragile to me, easily lost and by that fact precious.

Pammy's life feels that way to me too; and yours. I pray for Pammy every day; and I pray for you, as my Grandma taught me to pray: Take care of them all, Lord, I pray. Take care of Pammy and Myrna and Alix. Take care of my daughter Margaret, far away in London. Take care of Tildy, who is taking tap-dancing lessons—at her age!—and could quite easily break something. Take care of my brothers and their families. Take care of Nathan and Elinor in Atlanta. . . .

As if I thought the Lord couldn't find them unless I told Him where they were.

On and on. A long list.

Take care of me.

Honestly. Every day.

Sometimes I think I'm getting as nutty as Tildy.

And I pray for that baby on the bus. Do you remember that baby? That I told you about? Whatever became of her? Him? Did she—he—become a saint? Or a martyr?

Or just folks, like you and me?

How do we live from day to day? Why—we live by God's courtesy, in the shadow, or in the light, of our own deaths.

THE WEEKEND GIRL

I am a paid companion on weekends for an old lady who lives just across the river in St. Paul. The old lady's name is Sara. The time that I spend with Sara is boring. I nearly expire of boredom sometimes. But I am fond of her nevertheless.

Sara's memory is gone. We say the same things to each other over and over.

At the breakfast table:

Look what I've got for you, Sara. I say. (What I have is her medications: four little pills in the a.m., three at lunch, and three more at supper.)

Oh, aren't you sweet! says Sara. I forgot again. Aren't you dear!

Sara pretends that she is in charge and can be expected to remember things. Well: maybe *pretends* is the wrong word. Maybe she really believes it. I guess she does.

Yup, I say: You forgot again.

Lemon, vanilla, and coconut, I say. And chocolate. Your favorite.

My favorite is chocolate! Sara chirps.

Chocolate is your favorite! I echo, mindlessly.

Chocolate.

I think of Anthony, who loved chocolate, was absolutely mad for it: I sent him a card once that said: Things Are Getting Worse—Please Send Chocolate. And I am back in the dream of an hour ago, fast asleep in a bedroom of Sara's house. I dream that I am in a speedboat on a lake with Anthony. Really—in the real world—Anthony is dead. But in my dream he is steering the boat. Somewhere out on the water, there is an enemy. Well: and the water is in a way an enemy too. We can drown in the water: I know this in the dream. Anthony makes the boat go faster and faster. The edge of the boat dips nearer to the water with every turn. Anthony circles farther and farther out. He comes closer and closer to the enemy. We are in danger. *We are in terrible danger.*

* * *

Sweet. Sara says I am sweet. Can you imagine? I am about as sweet as strychnine. If Sara could see the inside of me sometimes, she would flinch in terror. She would run from me screaming. As, I imagine, I would from her. In my mind I am a murderer. Sometimes. But, of course, I can't be an off-again, on-again murderer: either I am one or I'm not. A thought is a thought. There's no taking a thought back. So: in my mind I am a murderer.

I can see inside of you, Sara says to me. Her head is tilted to one side, like a bird's. Sara, altogether, *is* like a bird: tiny, bony, nimble, quick. Winged. And—now that I am thinking of it—bird-brained too. What they say: a real feather-head.

Christ. Some people will make a joke out of anything; I am such a smartass.

You are good and sweet inside, she says. I know about these things.

I don't like that other person, she says. Who comes sometimes.

Lois. She doesn't like Lois: the five p.m. to nine a.m. weeknights person.

That other person—it's a terrible thing to say (says Sara)—she's inferior. Inside. You can tell. I can tell.

Well. Funny. That's just what I've always thought about Lois. Yes. But I never had the nerve to say it.

Because Lois is so kind and warm and energetic. On the outside.

* * *

I suspect she takes drugs.

Or drinks secretly.

Perhaps shoplifts.

Something.

* * *

It's a good day for Sara, I guess—that she remembers even that there *is* another person. *A good day?* No. We have had a good moment. The day can change at any second.

* * *

My, it looks cold, says Sara, staring out the window one morning at breakfast. All mornings.

It's thirty-five degrees, I say: quite warm for December, actually. (I have checked the indoor-outdoor thermometer, so I know this.)

Oh, she says, nods her head, looks wise: Yes, that's warm for December.

She stares out the kitchen window again.

My, it looks cold outside, she says.

Mmm, I say. Thirty-five degrees. Warm for December.

* * *

Nothing is stirring, she says. Look, nothing is stirring. There's not one breath of wind. Look.

The willow branches are moving a little, Sara, I say. See there?

I see, she says.

Pauses.
Nothing is stirring, she says.
It's so quiet. She says.
The willow is moving a little, I say.
Mm, she says. Pause.
Nothing is stirring, she says.
It's so quiet.

* * *

Oh. God. Folks?

I—my good inside screaming—I want to walk around the kitchen. I want to jump up and go into the den and grab a book, flop down and read. Or something. Bang my head on the wall. Something. Run out onto the street. Kill Sara. But I force myself to sit more or less still in my chair at Sara's breakfast table and I eat my breakfast. (The murderer sits at the table and eats my breakfast.)

Chomp. Chomp. Chomp. Look. My jaws are stirring. My teeth are crunching Bran Chex while Sara's rend an Eggo waffle.

* * *

I worry about the Wedgwood, Sara says.

The Wedgwood. I say.

Who shall I leave it to? says Sara. Who would care about it? And the silver? Who would care?

There's always someone, Sara, I say. In every generation. There's someone who cares about such things.

It's so quiet, she says.

Nothing is stirring.

She stares out the kitchen window. I stare. I see: the willow tree. A birdbath. Terraced lawn, sere now and brown, touched here and there with dirty snow. The deep white forgiving snow has not come yet this year. It is a brown December. In the newspaper they are predicting a brown Christmas. I see broken branches. A hose left out. Lonely and cold white metal chairs stacked on a table by the garage that attaches to this split-level house.

I worry *so* about the Wedgwood, Sara says. She turns her pretty, wrinkled face to me. Sara is eighty-two. She is absolutely serious now. Her eyes fill with tears. I worry about it all the time, she says.

Well, not all the time, I say. I laugh.

Sometimes you worry about the silver, I say.

* * *

Are the children in bed? she says.

Um—what shall I answer?

I answer nothing.

Where are the children? she persists.

I feel positively persecuted.

Uh, I say.

Where are they?

Oh my god, she is getting agitated. We tremble at the edge of disaster.

Where are my children?

Leave it alone, Sara . . .

Where?

Your children are grown and don't live here any more, Sara, I say. They have their own houses.

Grown? she says. That's crazy. You are lying. Why are you lying to me?

A wild, intense look comes into her eyes. I feel a little afraid of her. Sara, I see, is a murderer too.

Where is Trevor? she says.

Orient her to reality, they say: the people at the center that employs me.

So. Shall I tell her that her husband is dead? For ten years now? More? More than ten?

No. I shall not. Not this time. I shall have peace this time.

I don't know, Sara, I say. I don't know where Trevor is. I haven't seen him.

Not a lie: you'll grant that, surely?

* * *

I worry *so* about the Wedgwood, Sara says. Her face crinkles with anxiety. I get up from my chair. I kneel down beside her, I take her thin little body in my arms and hug her bones. It's all right, Sara, I say. Everything is all right. Don't think about the Wedgwood. Think about having a nice breakfast. Here. Now. With me.

I rub her back. Bones. She is nothing now but bones. A little sack of skin and fragile bird bones. My dear little bird-Sara. Whom I see on weekends for money.

Not a lot of money. Not enough. I figured it out the other day and came to the conclusion that I am spending two hundred dollars a month more than I earn. Something will have to give soon. I mean. I can't live on air. I can't live on nothing. There are things I have to buy. Why: there are even things I *want*...

* * *

Anthony—who was in my dream, do you remember him? —owned a very valuable piano the whole time I knew him, which was from the summer of 1953 until his death fifteen years ago.

My friend Elinor is—was—Anthony's wife. I knew Anthony almost as long as Elinor did. In fact, you could say that I met him on their honeymoon, since they had been married only three weeks when I went out to stay with them in New York. I was Elinor's student at the University of Minnesota and she let me come to New York and live with them: can you imagine it?

And Elinor and Anthony had known each other only three

weeks when they got married. Thus: Elinor knew Anthony six weeks longer than I did.

And Anthony had a piano.

It was a Steinway grand piano, full size. Big, folks. Somehow Elinor and Anthony had got it moved into a second-floor apartment in New York's Greenwich Village—on Morton Street, in a building which was subsequently bugged in connection with the McCarthy business: that circumstance seemed so romantic to me. This was where they lived when I visited them. The piano took up a whole room. I remember a room with nothing in it but that piano, its bench, and a glass table.

Oh, wait. I am forgetting the bear.

There was also a little wooden bear, perched on top of the piano. I recall the bear now that I am seeing that room in my memory: a carved bear maybe six or seven inches tall, seated at a little wooden piano. There was a handle attached to the little piano, and strings tied to the bear's paws were laced through the wooden keyboard and came out at the bottom of the piano. Tied to the ends of the strings—which were knotted together—was a wooden ball, maybe three-quarters of an inch in diameter. And—this is the big deal—when you picked up the whole apparatus by the handle and moved it gently in a circle, the ball swung and the strings pulled and released, pulled and released the bear's paws and—can you see this? god!—the bear played the little piano.

The first time I saw that bear, I was just knocked out.

Oh, I said.

I want that bear. I said. I must have that bear.

For heaven's sake, said Elinor. You can't have that bear. That's Anthony's bear. Don't you ask him for it either.

Anthony loves that bear. She said.

* * *

Elinor and Anthony moved fairly often over the years: eventually down to Atlanta, Georgia, where Elinor found a job teaching. Anthony didn't work at all except now and then as a piano tuner, and you can tune pianos anywhere, so Anthony went where there was work for Elinor and the piano went along.

There were two moves in Atlanta: from near the Spelman campus where Ellie taught, to the apartment across from Piedmont Park; and then to the house on Beech Valley Road that they finally bought.

It must have been a nightmare every time, moving that huge, sensitive thing, that piano. I mean, you'd think twice before you moved at all, if you had to take that piano along. Or, I would imagine you'd think twice.

One time—Ellie told me—they had to remove the frame of a second-story window and hire a crane to swing the piano through the hole and then they had to replace the frame and the window. Think of the expense. I *mean*.

* * *

When I was visiting them in Atlanta one summer they got the piano insured. They had been talking about doing it for a long time and they finally got to the point of calling an insurance agent. It was mostly Ellie's idea. I don't think Anthony believed in insurance. It was hard to tell what Anthony did believe in.

Kindness. Maybe kindness.

It was a funny sort of kindness, though. I mean, Anthony certainly wasn't kind to everybody.

The insurance agent came to the apartment to take a look at the piano. This was, I think, the Piedmont Park apartment, across from a little lake where ducks swam in the summertime.

What is it worth? the insurance man said. In your opinion?

How can I tell you that? said Anthony. It's worth millions to me.

But practically speaking, what dollar value would you set on it?

Practically speaking, it's priceless, said Anthony.

It's my life. He said.

The poor insurance man. He kept on, you have to give him credit for perseverance.

But what would such a piano cost if you went down and bought it at a store?

You couldn't buy this piano in a store, said Anthony.

Store! He laughed. Anthony's laughter was like bubbles coming up through lava: viscous, knowing, old as God.

But a piano *like* this, said the man.

There is no other piano like this, said Anthony. There is only this piano. My piano.

Nothing is stirring...

We've got to set a price, said the man. I appreciate your point of view. But we have to set a value. Or you can't insure it.

It's my wife who thinks we should insure it, said Anthony, shooting a mean look at Ellie. I don't want to insure it at all.

Your wife is absolutely right, said the insurance man. A valuable piece like this should be insured. What if you lost it in a fire? What amount of money would replace it?

It is irreplaceable, said Anthony.

Anthony—dead now, and one should not speak ill of the dead, but still—Anthony could be such an impossible shit.

* * *

Finally they set a dollar amount. It was a lot. I think it was ten thousand dollars. Something like that. And they got the piano insured.

The poor guy, said Elinor. I felt sorry for him. She said. How could you be so mean, Anthony?

I wasn't being mean, said Anthony. I just wanted him to see the truth: the piano is priceless.

Why didn't you try to see his truth? said Elinor.

Anthony's eyes—pale brown and limpid and innocent as death—widened for a second.

What truth did he have? he said.

Was it inconceivable that an insurance rep could have a truth? Apparently so.

That everything has a price. Said Elinor.

* * *

About now I imagine that you are wondering who and what Anthony is that he has this grandiose piano and does not appear to work at a job like the rest of us.

Well, yes, it is a puzzle, isn't it? But it has an answer. Of sorts. What passes for an answer.

Anthony was—before World War II—a sensitive, delicate, charming man, trained as a concert pianist, a real artist, who was—of course, what else?—among the first draftees into the army after the U.S. entered the war.

I have a snapshot of him from this period; he is dressed in a leftover uniform from World War I, tin helmet perched on his head and wrapped puttees on his legs; that's how early in the war it was, they didn't even have new uniforms yet, they had to make do.

Anthony wasn't in the army very long—a few months, maybe—but long enough to have a grand mal seizure one day and to be released from the service with a medical discharge and a full pension.

* * *

Suddenly a parallel with my own father strikes me, I wonder why I did not see it before; probably for the same reason that one lives behind one's nose and does not directly see it for a whole lifetime. My father was also educated as a concert pianist and sent to fight in World War I, until Vietnam the worst war of all, and was spit back into civilian life a couple of years later, less, as a destroyed human being.

My father and Anthony met once. Afterward my father said to me: that is a man who understands pain.

Ellie also said something like that. I asked her once: How come Anthony likes Holly so much? Holly was a person for whom at that time I personally would not have given you a quarter: I considered her—what a snob I was, I hate to write this next bit because it tells you so much about me—I considered her shallow and frivolous, a truly negligible human being.

Anthony sees the pain in her, said Ellie. And: Anthony is a barometer for pain.

I could never see Holly quite the same again.

When you look for the pain, you see things quite differently.

Anyway, that's why Anthony had the piano, and why he didn't actually have to work very much.

And Elinor worked. She was a professor of English at a college in Atlanta. Just so *somebody* works.

* * *

I took my daughter Margaret to visit Elinor and Anthony in Atlanta once. She was eleven years old at the time, and difficult.

She and Anthony took to each other at once. I mean, truly, they just fit together, like a hand and a glove. Love at first sight: I had never seen it before, but I believed in its possibility after that. Love at first sight can happen: I know that now.

Among other things, he taught her to play chess. Ellie and I marveled: impatient Anthony, who didn't like children at all as far as anyone could tell, and who revered chess. Anthony teaching chess to a child: why, we were amazed, Elinor and I.

She is very intelligent, he said, looking up at me once from a game.

She could be a good chess player. He said.

God: the highest accolade of all.

And Margaret—whose difficult heart was parched for approval—drank it up. You could see it happening: her heart became a sponge and soaked up the life-giving summertime drops of praise and saved them up for the years of winter that it knew were coming.

Anthony is simply wonderful, she whispered to me aside once.

Do you, um, do you think he, um, means it Mama, about me being smart?

Sure he means it, Margaret, I said. Can you imagine Anthony lying? About such a thing? I mean, Anthony almost can't lie, Margaret . . .

Anthony can't lie, she murmured.

He also played the piano for her: every day, for hours. Scarlatti. Cole Porter: "Smoke Gets in Your Eyes." Chopin. She sat beside him on the piano bench and bathed in floods of music, made just for her. Her face—so pretty, so closed—opened for him as a flower opens for summer.

This note here, he said. Hear this? He struck one note on the piano: Do you hear what this one note does? He played the note in a phrase, and then added another phrase.

I do see, she said. It makes it, it makes it possible . . . to . . . go on . . . it makes all the rest of it possible. . . .

Anthony laughed. He was so delighted with her. His slow, thick laughter bubbled up from his chest, like drowning. Right, he said. You do see it.

You try it now, he said. So she played the first phrase, and then the second one, flowing from the first.

You've got it, he said.

You're very bright, Margaret, he said. You're probably too bright. He put his hand over hers on the keyboard. Never let them tell you you're dumb. He said. Never; never.

* * *

I hear that piano sometimes. It plays Scarlatti in my head. It plays "Smoke Gets in Your Eyes." And sometimes I see the wooden bear: dipping and crouching, moving its arms, its paws, up and down, touching the wooden keys with wooden paws, a little wooden bear playing a little wooden keyboard. Tap, tap, tap. Rattatat. Tat. Playing, I guess you could say, a little wooden song. One note, of wood on wood: making everything else possible? What the hell: why not?

And I wonder sometimes how much of Margaret's subsequent life was given to her that summer by Anthony. You can't know. You can't ever know.

* * *

Sara taps her spoon on the edge of her orange juice glass and calls me back from memory.

Tap, tap, tap. Rattatat.

Back to work.

No woolgathering around old Sara.

Atten-*hut!*

* * *

Sara loves me, you know. In a funny kind of way, Sara loves me. And I love Sara.

In a funny kind of a way.

This is the way in which it is funny: Sara does not know me from one minute to the next. If you were to call on the phone and ask for me—*Is Joan there?*—she would tell you I was not there. If I was out of the room and she couldn't actually see me, she would tell you that she was alone.

It shakes up her children sometimes when she tells them she is alone. Perhaps they think I have flipped out at last and thrown in the towel and fled: maybe on the bus that runs on Cleveland Avenue two blocks away. Her children don't quite get the picture; to some extent they are still trying to believe that things are what they used to be, and that what Sara says can be relied upon. Well, it is hard for them. It is hard to watch a mind disintegrate; a personality dissolve. And so her children—Allan, Foster, and Mary Anne—pretend some of the time that nothing has changed.

Sara does not know my name. When I come to the door on Friday at 4:45 p.m. I am a stranger to her. Every Friday I must win her over again.

Hullo, Sara, I say when she opens the door to let me in.

Who are you? she says.

And yet, you know, when she sees me, each time, her little wrinkled face lights up. When she hears my voice, a question enters her mind, a puzzle: Who is this? Her mind has forgotten me, but her face remembers, and smiles.

What her face remembers is happiness. Sara is happy when she is with me. Sometimes. Not always. But sometimes.

To give someone happiness, even in a broken interval that will be forgotten five minutes later—thirty seconds later—is a way of loving them.

Thus: I love Sara. In a funny sort of way.

To accept happiness from another, even a broken-off shard of happiness that can never be stuck back onto a mended whole—is love also.

Thus: Sara loves me. In a funny sort of way.

* * *

I think it is possible, you know, that Sara is a much nicer person now than she was in her life.

In her life? Is this not her life then? Is walking around and saying words not life? Laughing? Is there no life here? None?

What I mean is this: all I ever hear concerning what she was like in earlier days is that she was a great hostess. Her husband, Trevor Hallingsgate, was a big gun at a large and important local company, a very highly respected industry, one so big it practically is the economy of the Twin Cities, Minneapolis and St. Paul; and so I guess you would have had to define her then as a company wife:

one of the great assets, as is now recognized, of an executive career, one of the essential components of a good man's rise.

Sara has closets jammed full of beautiful dresses. Evening gowns. Afternoon gowns. All of expensive and exquisite fabrics, all expensively made. Wonderful hand detailing. They are a bit out-of-date now, of course, but they are still very beautiful. Sara could wear them today and look okay.

Sometimes she does wear them. Sometimes she chooses a dress and puts on her furs and one of her children or grandchildren comes and gets her and drives her off in great style. The person who comes to get her always looks faintly embarrassed, however. Maybe she is overdressed? Dressed wrong? Inappropriately?

How would I know? I am just the weekend girl, and I cannot be expected to know about such things.

* * *

Sometimes I feel quite defensive in the midst of all this wealth and status. Well. Sometimes I feel quite defensive, period.

* * *

What was she like before all this began to happen? I asked her son Allan one day. Allan is Sara's younger son, and the one who does the most for her. Always one member of the family is chosen for this spot, have you noticed that? Usually it is a daughter, but in this family it is Allan, the younger son. In my own family it is me. My mother is in a nursing home in Northeast Minneapolis. I visit her once a week. For four or five hours: it's long enough. It's too long. I'm in worse shape when I come out of there than when I leave Sara. And *that*, God knows, is bad enough.

My mother was a wonderful hostess, Allan says.

She gave wonderful dinners and parties in this house.

Around that table. He points to the oval dining table under the crystal chandelier.

THE WEEKEND GIRL 183

She talked brilliantly, he says. She was up on everything. Whatever was going on she knew about. Information-wise, she was at the cutting edge. He says.

At the cutting edge. Wow. Hear that.

Information-wise.

Well, but it seems to me that there is more to her than that, I say. Than just a hostess. I get little clues. I mean, for example, was she ever interested in, say, metaphysics or anything like that? For example?

I was never aware of anything like that, he says. Frowns.

(Not *my* mother . . .

(Heavens to Betsy.)

* * *

Maybe you need to know something about me. Well. I am the teller of the story. Or stories. There are two of them, aren't there? Getting tangled up together: Anthony's story, and a story about Sara, who forgets everything and has to have a caregiver.

I told you that I am Sara's weekend girl. Woman. I am sixty years old, for heaven's sake. I am not a *girl*. Not any more: I was once. And I was Anthony's friend. The two stories come together in me. And the two people: they touch only in me. They never knew each other. You could say, I guess, that I am the crux of the matter.

My memory, my awareness, is where they live, have their simultaneous being.

And when I die, when I can no longer remember, if that's what happens, then are they gone too?

Well, no, maybe not. Maybe there is another memory; maybe God remembers.

I am someone who thinks such thoughts. Take it or leave it.

"You are God in your stories," says my best critic. I don't forget statements like that: People should be very careful what they say. I told you before that thoughts are real; well, words are real too.

So. A while ago I told you that I was a murderer. And now I tell you that I am God.

And I have a great many other identities, some of which are more peculiar still.

"You can do anything in your stories," says my critic. (Listen, I have a letter. I can prove that he actually did say this.) "In your stories, you are God. You can twist, turn, poke, relate apparently unrelated elements. Anything. You are God. You can do what you want to."

So that is what I am doing here. I am poking, twisting, pushing.

And here you thought I was just fooling around.

I used to be a social worker.

Before that I was a housewife. And a mother. A daughter.

I was good at all those things, in fact I was excellent.

But they didn't make me happy. They were not the right things for me to do, apparently.

So I gave them up.

When I could. As much as I could.

For this.

And what is this? Why, I am a drifter. A watcher. A teller of stories. Someone who loves Sara: sort of: and takes care of her. Someone who knew Anthony.

Someone who now and then dreams a strange dream in a bedroom in someone else's house.

So: a murderer. God. A story-teller. A sort of lover. A knower. A dreamer.

Closer to the bone, I think, all these things, than being a social worker. Or even a mother.

Do you know me now?

Well, but it isn't my fault. No one knows another. No story-teller is good enough to tell you who he is; not even God.

* * *

Nothing is stirring....
The wooden bear still sits on Anthony's piano, although Anthony is dead now fifteen years.

Every now and then Ellie has someone come in to play on the piano, so that the piano does not die. This is the truth, I am not making this up: things can die. The piano could die if no one played it. Honestly. Ask anybody. Well: any piano person.

* * *

Sara holds out her arms to me and tilts up her face to be kissed.

I am very fond of you, she says.

What would I do without you? she says. Tears spring to her eyes and spill.

I hold her in my arms and she cries and cries.

What is it, Sara? What's the matter? I say.

My husband is dead, she sobs. My mother is dead. My father is dead. My brother is dead.

I'm sorry, I say. I'm so sorry, Sara.

I'm all alone, she sobs.

Poor little Sara, I say. It's all right, Sara . . . it's all right . . . everything is going to be all right. . . .

And: You've got me, Sara: I say.

(You know that "Sara" is not her real name. I told her one day that I was writing a story about her, and she chose the name "Sara" for the story. And then a grandchild was born and they named the child "Sara" plus my Sara's real name. By accident. So you see how strange things are? And you can't complain if my story seems from time to time to be a little strange, too. . . .)

My Sara holds my hands tight. She peers up into my face. Her eyes are sad now and clear and naked, there is definitely someone inside, and her little face, tear-smudged, is like a washed flower.

How could I bear to live, she says, if you were not here to comfort me?

* * *

I can never leave her. You can see that.
I am so ashamed, she whispers.
People like Sara are not supposed to know enough about what's going on to be ashamed.
But they do.
Oh, my, yes, they do.
They know. Sara knows.
And is bitterly ashamed.
You don't need to feel ashamed, Sara, I say. You're a good, sweet person this minute, I say: that's all that's important.
But I don't remember things, she says. Important things. How could I forget such things? How could I forget that my husband is dead? What is wrong with me?
That doesn't matter, Sara, I say. That's a non-essential.
It is? she says.
It is, I say. Firmly. (What do I know? I am making it up by the yard now. Peace at any price. Comfort for my darling at any price.)
What is, dear? she says.
Memory, I say. Memory is a non-essential.
A non-essential, she repeats: memory is a non-essential.
She laughs.
Hm, she says.
I never thought of that. She says.
A non-essential.
Hm.

* * *

THE WEEKEND GIRL 187

Is it? I am asking you. Is memory a non-essential? What if you haven't got it? What are you? Are you human? Well. Are you *alive?* Listen, are you even . . . *there?* At all? Think about it: if you can bear to.

Borges—the Argentinean writer. Yes, I read. I am more than just a weekend girl. You thought I was just a weekend girl—Borges says that we *are* our memory.

* * *

After Anthony died, Elinor told me that she got depressed when she thought about his life. What did he *do?* she said; I mean, in his whole life, what did he actually *do?*

Do, I said. What do you mean, *do?*

Well, I mean, she said. People do things. Everybody does something. Anthony didn't have a real *job,* he didn't have a *career,* he didn't do *anything.* And he was, I believe, in his heart, terribly ashamed of that.

Ashamed, I said. But why on earth? I said.

Because he thought he wasn't a *man,* said Ellie. He thought that if you don't do what men do, support a family and all that, then you weren't a *man.*

He *was* something, I said. You don't have to *do* anything.

What was he, said Ellie.

He was a *person,* I said. He was a human being. . . .

You know perfectly well that doesn't count, said Ellie. She was terribly cross: my goodness, I was stepping on toes here, apparently.

Besides, I said.

Another thing. I said.

Who did he hurt? You can hurt a lot of people with all this *doing.* . . .

* * *

Sara is watching "Nova" one day on the TV. I am sewing. Hand sewing is one of the things I do at Sara's to keep from going completely crazy.

Does it ever seem to you, dear, she says, that sometimes things start to happen in your mind and then they come out somewhere else? Later? In the world?

Oh, in the world, I say. Sure, Sara. I guess so. Why not? It could work that way. . . .

She persists.

I mean, that you can see how things are going to be in the world because there's a picture of it now?

Sure, I say. Okay. I sort of almost see what she is getting at. I mean: sort of. I sort of do. Don't you?

Actually, she is probably getting worse; that is probably what is happening. Her condition, as they say, is deteriorating. She is—as they also say—decompensating.

* * *

Sara is now into what they call the third stage of Alzheimer's disease. This is the worst and final stage. At least, this is what they say now. God knows what they might say tomorrow. They change their minds about these things, you know. You can't afford to believe them entirely, ever.

For example, after I had been working with Sara for about a year, they changed their minds about Orienting To Reality. No, no, they suddenly said: Don't Do That After All, That Is Totally Wrong.

Instead, you are now supposed to validate whatever is the reality of the person who has Alzheimer's. We do not any more tell Sara that Trevor is dead, for example. Instead we make up huge stories about this hunting trip up north that he is supposed to be on.

Sara gets a little pissed that he is on a hunting trip—*again?!!*—but nowhere near as upset as she got the one time

I told her he was dead: the time I had to lock myself in the bathroom in the middle of the night for three hours.

The party line now is to lie to her. Well. I could have told them a long time ago that lying was the right track.

Validation Therapy, they call it.

* * *

You know, I am definitely getting nuttier as I get older. The things that interest me are getting stranger and stranger. I mean, even I have to admit it. Take for example the business of the napkins.

I save paper napkins. To recycle.

Well, it makes some sense. Unless you absolutely maul them, unless you are eating barbecued ribs or fried chicken or something, napkins are usually perfectly good after you've used them. Most of the time. Aren't they? You have to admit I'm right.

I have been recycling them for at least fifteen years now. I began when I was still a social worker. People absolutely hated it. People got really upset. Well: it is such a crazy thing to do, isn't it?

Recycling as what? someone said to me once, making a face. A brave person. Most people are afraid to ask.

Well, as anything. Obviously. In any situation where you might have used a small bit of new paper, to wipe up a spill, say. For example.

Isn't that obvious?

Maybe not. The most deeply held secrets of the human soul are the little ones, the silly ones, that are so little and so peculiar that no one would ever, ever guess them. Never. Ever.

I recycle paper napkins is much harder to say than *I am a murderer*. Well, you have no idea how I worked myself up to tell you this about myself, that I am a napkin-saver. (Shall I? Can I? Oh, gosh. What will they think. Etc. Etc.) Being a murderer has some class. Saving napkins is just peculiar.

It's okay to be different, someone said: it's not okay to be peculiar.

I have to admit that recycling napkins borders on peculiar; or goes right over the edge.

But everybody does peculiar things. Lots of people anyway. Maybe not everybody. But take for example my friend Maeve's sister Edith. Maeve told me once that Edith saves old cardboard tubes from toilet paper rolls and stuffs them full of snotty kleenexes and uses them to help start the fire in the fireplace. This she does in the name of ecology. But I know the truth: a limited truth, but nevertheless a truth: she may have done it at first because of an idea about ecology—saving trees, I guess, I mean that is why I recycle napkins, to save trees —but after a while she did it, now she does it, simply for the clear, pure, uncomplicated joy of stuffing used kleenexes into old t.p. tubes. *I know this.*

* * *

(Well. Of course I started stuffing t.p. tubes as soon as I heard about it. But something awful happened. I began to use more kleenexes so that I could stuff the tubes faster.

(Ditto napkins. I probably use more napkins now so that I can recycle them.

(So you see, it is *plain* crazy, there is *absolutely no sense in it.*)

* * *

Sara is a paper napkin saver too. But she makes no pretense about recycling the napkins, she just saves them because she likes them so much.

I discovered this one day when we both spied her crumpled napkin, left from lunch, lying on the little tray table by the sofa in the family room.

We eat our meals, usually on two tray tables, one for her and one for me, in the family room facing the TV. Three meals a

THE WEEKEND GIRL 191

day, three clean paper napkins. Each. Three each. So with luck I can recycle six napkins a day.

So anyway, there is this napkin lying lonely on Sara's tray table. Both of our hands reach out simultaneously to grab it. And stop, stuck in midair.

She looks at me.

I look at her.

Guilt is written all over her face. So is it I suppose on mine.

She speaks first, it is after all her napkin.

There is a protocol in matters such as this as well as in the larger matters of the world.

You like them too: she says.

Oh, yes, I do: I say.

You take it, she says.

No, no, I say: It's yours.

She sits down by the little tray table. She moves the napkin into the perfect center of the table. She smooths it flat. Corrects its position a tiny bit. She has forgotten all about me. She is lost in admiration.

Isn't it nice, she says.

Oh.

Isn't it *soft*. . . .

Oh, isn't it *square*. . . .

Her little hand, still delicate and lovely, her little white fingers with pink-painted, manicured nails—her kids take her to the beauty shop once a week for nail and hair repairs, etc., they do their best to keep her up to scratch—her hands flutter like birds over the napkin. Pat, pat. Oh. Soft . . . oh. Square. Ahhh. . . .

She remembers me then.

Looks at me and smiles.

You take it, she says.

Sara! I say: I couldn't. Not that one. That's yours.

I want you to have it, she says: truly. Her crazy and faded eyes through which the murderer looks out sometimes, her eyes are gentle at this moment, generous, loving.

I want you to have it. She says.

Well, I am so touched. Oh, Sara, I say. God. Thank you. Thank you.

I take it. I fold it up and add it to the three others in my pocket.

Thank you, Sara, I say. It's a really nice present.

Yes, she says.

It is. She says. Isn't it.

* * *

Later on the same weekend, I am opening drawers looking for her house key, which she has somehow lost and is obsessively seeking.

I find a drawer that is full to the top with used paper napkins. Sara's secret stash.

I won't tell you where mine is.

Not long ago I said to a friend—the same friend, Maeve, whose sister stuffed the t.p. tubes—I said, Do you think I'm crazy?

We were talking about my recycling activities. Or my napkin recycling project. Many years have gone by and I have expanded a great deal from the original project—I now try to recycle everything recyclable. I expect I *have* gotten kind of nuts.

Do you think I'm crazy?

Well, yeah, said Maeve. A little. But who are you hurting?

Yes. Put *that* in your pipe and smoke it. Who am I hurting?

* * *

I think of Anthony playing "Smoke Gets In Your Eyes" for Margaret, telling her she was smart. I suspect, you know that Margaret lived for years, like a camel, like a cactus in the desert, on the life-giving idea that Anthony gave her.

I think of the bear, playing its wooden song. Around, around, around, the little wooden ball goes, on the little strings: and the wooden paws rise, fall, rise, fall, plock plock plock....

A wooden song....

Whose hand is moving the wooden paddle in a circle, swirling the wooden ball? I see the bear in my memory, you know, often; but I never see the hand.

I never see the hand.

* * *

I can't leave Sara. How could I leave her? But I have to find some way to make another two hundred dollars a month. Maybe I could sell the napkins? To make back into trees? Isn't there someone, somewhere, who can make old napkins into trees? Two hundred dollars a month doesn't seem excessive for all my napkins.

* * *

I suppose you think I can work somewhere else too, in addition to working with Sara. Maybe with another old lady? Well, no—I can't. You don't understand; that is clear.

I mean, Sara tears me apart. Sara wipes me out. Absolutely. When I leave her house on Monday morning, I am too crazy to live. Much less work any more. It takes me three days to recover from the weekend with Sara.

* * *

When I sit in Sara's living room during the time I take care of her—Friday night and Saturday and Sunday until early Monday morning—I feel sometimes that my life is pouring away, is being wasted. Well, not wasted, exactly, I am after all doing some good here, am I not? but, well, *pouring away*. That's nearest. Like sand down a rathole, as they say. Like spilt milk flowing: *away*.

And I begin to think strange thoughts. I think that if this is all that's left after you take away people and activity and complex interaction and, you know, art and music and walking around the lake and having a cat, or a kid, if *this,* sitting in Sara's living room watching TV and feeling *poured away,* is *it,* why then life doesn't amount to a hill of beans. Not to zip shit. See?

And I think: but I am making a living here. And then I get caught on that: making a living. Making. A. Living. Now: what does *that* mean? I mean, isn't that an absurdity?

I laugh out loud.

What is it, dear? says Sara.

Nothing, Sara, I say.

I can't even try to tell her about it, because she doesn't know that I am paid. She thinks that I come here for love's sake. Because I am a friend. How else would you, logically, explain to yourself someone else's presence in your house? In your life?

I was just laughing at, uh, something funny that went through my mind, Sara, I say.

What, she says.

Well, I don't know any more, I say. I don't remember.

Does that ever happen to you, Sara? I say.

(Oh, clever . . .)

She laughs.

Oh, my, she says. Oh, yes.

A wry and bitter look twists her mouth for a second. For a second she is really in there. I can see *her* in her eyes.

* * *

Sara closes her eyes and goes back to snoozing, which is what she mostly does these days.

I am alone again, and slow lazy crazy thoughts float in and out. Again.

When I was a child, I used to—when I was very tired, it only happened when I was very tired—I used to place a chair in my mind. A plain straight-backed wooden kitchen chair. Like the chairs in our kitchen in the old house on Sheridan Avenue in Minneapolis: round-backed, with wood slats.

Once I was playing "train" with my brothers and I got my legs stuck in one of those chairs and I couldn't get out, my Daddy had to actually saw the chair off of me. Now I have those chairs in the basement of my house on Bryant Avenue in South Minneapolis, and I have only three of them, because one was sawed up.

And I would place one of those plain wooden kitchen chairs into my mind when I was very tired. I would do it deliberately, because I knew that what would happen would be pleasant. What would happen is this: the chair would begin to dissolve. I would see all the little atoms and molecules or whatever in the chair and they would be made of light and I would think—softly, lazily—my goodness, the chair is made of light.

Pieces of light.

And the pieces of light would, like, move around? So that inside of itself the chair would be very busy, very lively. But soft—oh—very, very soft, and, and, you know, *slow?* Well, I can't tell you. But there has never been anything else so soft. So slow. Unless it was semen, the slip-slidey feel of semen? But I was a child, I couldn't call it semen, could I?—the chair is *soft*, I thought. The chair is *slow* . . .

Slip-slidey. . . .

And then the soft pieces of light would start to sort of flake off, fall off? And the chair would be *getting smaller* . . . ah God. The very nicest feeling: like everything was going away. . . .

I would fall asleep, always, before the chair was all gone.

So I never knew whether the chair would disappear altogether. I always tried to stay awake to see, but I never could.

What was I talking about? Sara: I have slip-slid away from Sara's living room.

Well. Here I am again, sitting in Sara's living room. And I am suddenly depressed as I sit here, next to Sara, on the blue couch looking out through the picture window onto the patio. I see the dirty brown snow: a brown Christmas, I think. . . .

* * *

Nothing is stirring. . . .

* * *

My life is getting smaller as I sit here, is becoming infinitely cramped and drawn in upon me. Aarghh—I am choking on life. My life is smothering me. God. God.

Is it like this for her?—I wonder, as I drown in the last piece of my life.

Oh. The world is squeezing in on me. Smaller and smaller and smaller and smaller, I am getting smaller, like Alice, I have drunk from the poisoned bottle that says Drink Me, I am certainly going to die soon . . . one of these days. . . .

Sara! I say. I jump up. I have a great idea. Let's go outside. Let's walk.

Oh, it's too cold, says Sara, startled awake.

It's not, I say. It's really very mild for this time of year.

What time of year is it? says Sara.

It's almost Christmas, Sara, I say.

Christmas? she says. Her eyes flare.

Oh, oh, oh, a mistake, oh god. She'll start to worry now. About gifts, for example. About cards. Cookies. She'll get crazy. But she loses it. Sometimes I luck up.

It looks cold, she says.

I breathe again. It's pretty warm, Sara, I say. Thirty-four degrees. Warm for December.

It's.

Warm.

For.

December.

* * *

The first time I ever laid eyes on Anthony was in Grand Central Station.

Honestly. This is not a joke.

I mean: Grand Central Station. Anything about G.C.S. sounds like a joke. To me it does. Like Cucamonga is always a joke. Or Anaheim. Remember: if you are old enough: *Anaheim . . . Azuza . . . and Kook . . . amongaaaaa. . . .* The train conductor calling stops on Jack Benny's radio program: *Anaheim . . . Azuza. . . .*

You're probably not old enough.

Well, anyway.

I got off the train from Minneapolis: the Super Chief? I think it was called the Super Chief, that train: after twenty-eight of the most miserable hours I ever spent in my life up to then. Subsequently, I have spent many, many hours that were much worse than that: in marriage, childbirth, parenthood, employment, divorce, life-in-general, you name it; but at that time I was young. I didn't know.

It was during some war, I think—maybe the Korean?—and the train was crowded with servicemen. There were too many people in the car I was in —some of them had to sit on their suitcases in the aisle, they swayed and caught themselves with every bend of the track. How could they do that for twenty-eight hours, I thought? I was so lucky, I had a seat. My father had got that for me. He took me to the station that morning and checked my bags and looked up the conductor of the train and introduced me to him: This is my little girl, he said. She thinks she knows it all. She's going off to Sodom. New York City. You will take care of her for me, sir? Yes sir, said the conductor. I'll surely do that.

And of course I never saw him again.

Anyway. I was twenty-two. I was just out of college with a

brand-new B.A. in English in my pocket, and top honors. I did know it all. I had my worldly goods—all of them—packed in two big suitcases. And I had a new hat. I was all set. The plan was to take New York by storm—of course, it wasn't going to work out, but I didn't know that, did I?

That hat: I will never forget that hat. If I live to be as old as Sara, I'll *never* forget that hat. (Well, unless of course I forget everything, as Sara has. In that case I probably won't remember the hat. But you know what I mean: if I've got my marbles at all, I'll remember that hat.)

What a wonderful hat it was! It was fitted close to my head, like a Juliet-cap, tapering toward the back and dipping down in front to a shallow point, so that it made my face into a heart. The crown of it was made of stiff black velvet, but a little white straw band shaped the heart-point in front and narrowed back toward my ears. And a crisp black veil came just to the tip of my nose, so that the things I thought were disfiguring about my face—the family nose and my glasses—were hidden a little, were softened.

That hat was a magic hat. The minute I tried it on in the store, I knew it for magic: with that hat on I was sleek, elegant, poised, soignée. Without it, I was just me: skinny, depressive, awkward, self-conscious and almost paralyzed with fright. The B.A. degree said that I was something I wasn't: which is to say, ready. All set. Prepared. The hat said, Ready or not, here I come! The hat said I was okay. Oh. Kay. Definitely.

Isn't it marvelous what a *hat* can do? Something that little? How lucky you are, my husband – ex – said once: *You can go and buy something so little, and you're okay? How lucky you are!*

Well, yes, I *am* lucky.

I have always been lucky in that way.

People who are made happy by very small things *are* lucky, don't you think? There are so many small things: shoes and cabbages and sealing wax. Chessmen. Paper napkins. Wooden bears.

Ships and kings are bigger.

So anyway there I am, getting off this grungy, dirty, hot and uncomfortable train after sitting up for twenty-eight hours. *I am so dirty; I feel so dirty.* Suddenly I know that I have made a mistake and I am not going to stay here. Panic sets in.

Also I know suddenly that I have brought too much stuff. Much too much. I am ludicrous, that's what I am. Those two huge suitcases. New. Everyone will look at those new suitcases and they will know that I am a hick from the Midwest. Everyone will just look at me, one look, that is all it will take. What a hick, everyone will say. In unison: all these loud fast knowing people around me on the platform: *What a hick!*

Anthony will say. And here they are. Here she is. Ellie, my teacher: my dear, my beautiful friend; and next to her is, I can't believe this person.

Can this be Anthony? This?

He is very short, no taller than me, which I am five feet five inches tall. Or I was then, I am beginning to shrink. It is too soon for me to shrink. I think it is.

He is very homely, he has a terrible skin problem, acne or something, he is skinny and small and he has this mouth that sort of, you know, hangs open? I mean, like an idiot, I swear to God.

This is the person that my darling, my so charming Elinor, has married? I am, yes, dumbstruck. Struck dumb.

Then he looks at me, really *looks*. I mean, nobody really looks at anybody, do they? But Anthony looks at me, and he *sees me*, I feel truly *seen*, maybe for the first time ever, and then he smiles, a wonderful, gay crazy smile; and he laughs, that bubbling laugh of his from deep inside where something is so funny and so sad, both at the same time, that knowing, painful laugh;

those limpid and innocent brown eyes *see me;* and he says, Ellie, you didn't tell me she was beautiful.

Well, Christ. You'd be his slave for life too, wouldn't you? If you were me? Sure you would.

If you were me.

* * *

The dream I had at Sara's house, the dream of Anthony and me in the boat, was nearly a nightmare. Well: insofar as any dream I have is nightmare—mostly I just stand back in my dreams and watch and comment; sort of like what happens in my waking life—but with that reservation, surely that dream was nightmare.

"Nightmare"—I have just now gone to the dictionary, I am caught by the word: *night* I can get, but *mare?* and the dictionary says that this mare is not the horse kind, rather it is from the Icelandic *mare* meaning an evil spirit that comes in dreams—my dream was a nightmare.

There *was* an evil spirit in it: but what could that spirit have been? Pain? I told you that Anthony was a barometer for pain. Evil? The knowledge of good and evil? In the garden?

I am looking at Sara's garden now, out her picture window: the bleak brown grass, the useless hose that should have been taken in, the stacked chairs. In the summer the garden will be beautiful: men will come, and women, gardeners, and they will prune and plant and mow and stake, and in one day the garden will be transformed.

Danger: that's what the dream said, didn't it? *There is danger here.*

That dream cries out for interpretation, said Elinor when she read this story last summer. Well, not by me, Ellie, I haven't, as they say, got a clue.

Danger, danger, danger: ding, dong, ding, dong: ringing out like an alarm bell.

***

We walked back to the Morton Street apartment, Ellie and Anthony and me, that night I arrived in New York City, only a few blocks, not worth getting a cab for, they said, and you couldn't find a cab anyway at that time of night, and Anthony insisted on carrying both of those two heavy bags of mine, and Anthony was so short that the biggest bag barely skimmed the sidewalk at every step and he walked ahead, charging ahead of us with those suitcases, being a man, taking care, and we followed him; and something about that little, little man, seen from the back, bumping along the dark streets of the Village with those heavy suitcases, *I did bring too much stuff, I am ludicrous,* something about it, him, touched me, wounded me, in a place so deep inside, so delicate, that I was hurt forever. In that place I will feel pain forever. I will remember it forever.

Well: unless I forget it, I guess.

Like Sara. I can never say anything anymore without thinking of Sara. It is like Sara is changing the categories of my mind.

Has Sara forgotten something like that?

No. No. Absolutely not. Not like that. Surely. No.

And who am I to think that her memories are not as special as mine?

Who am I?

I can't tell you.

I can't tell you, dear. And that is another deep and terrifying pain.

***

My daughter took a class in astronomy once. At one point she was full of the chaos theory, or it could have been The Big Bang, something like that, anyway she said that according to that theory we are all of us tenth-generation (or millionth— what do *I* know?) *star-stuff.* I can't tell you how completely that notion grabbed me, and held me: well, you probably have already grasped the idea that anything *odd* enough will grab me, hold me.

I've been hanging on to that notion for at least ten years, wanting to put it into a story, and hey, here it is now.

Another notion: a man I know refers to himself—whenever he talks at all, which sometimes seems non-stop—as a Child of God. "I am an alcoholic and a Child of God," he says. After a while it ceases to be startling and becomes a commonplace: Oh, there's old Bob, he's a Child of God. . . .

Another school of thought—I can hear you saying it, "This is *thought?*"—says that we are, all of us, angels, souls, made of light in our real selves. Like my chair—wow! *made of light.* So: star-stuff, Child of God, angel, soul, light—under any of those flags I am clearly mandated, it seems to me, to behave as well as I can.

My friend Maeve that I told you about before told me a funny story once: she was yelling at her son, Mike, when he was a kid: Michael, *behave yourself. Behave!*

And Michael said: Mama, I'm *being* have. . . .

So: God, I'm being have. I'm doing the best I can, as clearly as I can see The Best.

* * *

Anthony.

For that matter, who was Anthony?

One day when I was with Bud Shepherd—whom I subsequently married—in my apartment on the U of M campus, the phone rang, and it was Ellie.

Remember I told you about this guy I met, said Ellie over the phone, and that was how it all started.

Anthony, I said.

Yeah, she said. She laughed a little. Anthony. Ha-ha.

Yes? I said. Well?

We got married today, she said. I married him today.

She laughed again, a little tiny laugh, so like Elinor to laugh, she knew how much this news would amaze me.

I remember that I was standing with my back to the wall with the up-and-down striped burgundy and green and cream fleur-de-lysed wallpaper that I thought was so elegant, I absolutely loved that little apartment, it was my first place away from my parents' home, and it really was perfectly charming, and I slid down the wall quite deliberately until I was sitting on the floor. I did this on purpose, you must understand, I mean I didn't fall down or anything. I had to do something to express my absolute astonishment.

Poor old Bud looked quite frightened. I waved him away. Camille taking care of herself: I'm all right, Armand, it's nothing, really . . . nothing fatal. . . .

Amaze. How this would amaze me? Did I say? Hurt. Offend. Infuriate. That was more like it.

Are you still there? Ellie said.

Oh, I'm here, I said.

You didn't say anything, she said. I thought you'd *say* something.

You what, I said. You did what.

Got married, she said. I got married.

You got married, I said. I could hear my voice start to shrill. And you didn't *tell me?*

Ellie! You didn't tell me? I more or less shouted.

I mean, it was a kind of a game, you know. It wasn't entirely real. It was a kind of play-acting. I expect Ellie knew that; she always did know me pretty well.

The Mata Hari of Minneapolis, she called me once.

It was kind of sudden, she said.

Sudden, I said. You could have called me. Before.

Well, no, I couldn't, she said. It was sudden. We just decided to do it and we went down to city hall and we did it. . . .

Marriage isn't sudden, I said. You don't get married suddenly.

It is for me, she said. I did. She said.

You could have called, I said. You had a day. You had ten minutes. Before.

I was afraid to, Ellie said.

Afraid, I said. What of.

I was afraid you were going to take it like this, she said.

Like this, I said. Like how?

Like you're taking it, she said. Badly.

Suddenly she got mad at me: You have no right to take it badly, she said. You ought to be happy for me. You ought to wish me happiness. . . .

I do, I said. I do wish you happiness. I, I wish you *both* all the happiness in the world. . . .

Oh, yes, you sound like it, she said.

Ellie, I said. That's not fair. It's not fair to say that. I can't help how I sound. I do wish you happiness. Honestly I do.

My fingers are crossed: I wish you a quick divorce. I wish you. I am the bad fairy at the christening; I know it.

What about Larry? I said. What the hell happened to *Larry?*

Oh, Larry, Ellie said.

What do you mean, what happened to him.

I guess he's all right.

She said.

You were going to *marry* him, I said. You were for god's sake *engaged* to him. You had a *ring!*

Yes, well, I gave the ring back. . . .

That makes it all right, I suppose. . . .

Ellie started to giggle in this crazy way. If you could hear yourself, she said. You sound like my mother: *You had a ring.* . . .

And you sound like a tramp, I said.

Then she got mad again. Well, I don't blame her, do you?

A friend calls you a tramp on your wedding day? A pipsqueak student?

Listen, kid, these things happen, she said. For gosh sakes. What difference does it make to *you* anyway? Which one I married?

Yes, well, I was *used* to Larry, I said. I was used to that idea, that *some day* you would marry Larry....

It wouldn't have worked out, said Ellie. You are going to like Anthony a whole lot better than you ever would have liked Larry....

Sure, I said.

You are, said Ellie. I promise.

Can I come to New York, I said. Like I was going to.

Of course, said Ellie. Of course you can.

The bridegroom doesn't object? I said.

You can come, said Ellie.

Next month? Just like we planned?

Certainly, said Ellie.

Look, I've got to hang up, she said. I've got to hang up now....

Don't hang up, I said.

I have to hang up, she said.

Don't.

Bye. See you. I'll write to you.

Soon?

Soon.

Okay.

Bye-bye.

I hung up the phone.

Bad news, I guess, said Bud.

I looked at him. You're here? I said.

Well, sure I'm here, he said. I was here when the phone rang and I'm still here....

I looked at him, focused on him: dark, eagle face, dark hair, black eyes. Some Indian there. Good looking, people thought. Attractive. Oh, very. In that stand-offish way.

Do you want to get married? I said. And: How would you like to get married?

* * *

Living in the one-bedroom apartment on Morton Street either wasn't as bad as it seems to me it should have been, or else I was too young and too used to discomfort to care. I remember that I slept on a sort of day bed in the living room, pushed up against a wall. During the day, the bed was made up and functioned as part of the furniture of the room.

I suppose it is odd, or at least very unusual, that Elinor let me come out to stay with her and Anthony in that little apartment when they were first married. It didn't seem odd to me; I had all the egotism and self-absorption of extreme youth, and it seemed to me that this was what *should* happen, just because it was happening to *me*. Elinor was my teacher; I had hung out on the fringes of her pre-beatnik crowd at the University of Minnesota while she taught and got her doctorate; I don't know, I guess I felt that she had somehow saved my life and should have been on that account forever responsible for me.

Saved my life. That isn't too much of an exaggeration, you know—not too far off the mark. It was like she reached into the great pool of students on the swollen post-World War II campus and grabbed me as a piece of flotsam that might otherwise have simply sunk. She wouldn't let me sink. She put me up for one scholarship and prize after another; and, miracle! I won them all. For her. For her, I became a sort of prize-winning machine.

What I am trying to tell you is that she claimed me, she shaped me and made me, I was her creature as surely as I was God's.

One day recently I said to Maeve—you remember her, she is also a friend of Elinor's—Maeve, do you think I have an East

Coast accent? Or a British accent? People are always saying that I have. She thought it over quite carefully, her answer was careful: I think you talk like Elinor, she said. I think you have an Elinor accent.

* * *

I tried one day not long ago to tell Elinor about Sara.

Does she remember you? she asked. From weekend to weekend?

No, I said. Not exactly remember.

That is so strange, she said. It is really hard to even think about it. How long do you think her memory span is?

Well, it varies, I said.

Some things get stuck in her head and she talks about them all day. Many days.

Other things she remembers for maybe thirty seconds. Why: less. Two seconds. One.

And you have to keep saying the same things over and over? says Ellie. Answering the same questions?

Yes. I say. Over and over.

Doesn't it drive you crazy? she says.

Sure, I say. Absolutely. I get out of there, I'm a basket case.

Why do you do it? says Ellie. I think it's marvelous that you do it, but *why* do you do it? I mean, you're trained to do higher level things than this. . . .

Oh, yeah, I say. High level. Administrative stuff. Figuring out budgets. Supervising. Like that. That's what MSWs do now, you know. They don't really take care of people anymore. They do budgets. That really *would* drive me crazy. And in a much worse way.

This is better, I say. I know you don't understand it. I don't understand it either. But this is perfect for me.

This is a better kind of crazy.

* * *

The dream sticks in my mind that whole next day. I think about it while I am sitting on the blue couch, with Sara sitting next to me, both of us staring out the window at the dirty snow, the brown grass.

A brown Christmas, I think.

What could be worse than a brown Christmas?

Well, plenty of things, I say to myself. I mean, let's get a grip on ourselves here.

I try telling Sara about the dream. Well, it's a little better than talking to myself. It's a little better than talking to a, you know, a *post*.

And sometimes Sara surprises me. Sometimes she comes up with great things. Really wonderful. One day, for example, she says: apropos of nothing that I recall, she says: Most of living is bravery.

Most of living is bravery. I hugged her, and laughed, and told her how smart I think she is. My god, Sara, I said, that is *so good*. . . .

What is *so good*? she said.

What you said, Sara. That most of living is bravery. . . .

I never said that, she said.

I said that?

And: What does it mean?

She said.

* * *

So I tell her about the dream. We are going farther and farther out on the water, Sara, I say. Anthony is steering the boat faster and faster in big curves that dip the edge of the boat right down to the water, and I know we can drown, and out in the water is another danger. . . .

She is listening very carefully. She likes to be consulted on things. Her blue eyes are squeezed up and intent, she is trying so hard.

You loved him, dear, she says.

Oh, no, Sara, I say. That isn't it. He was my friend's *husband*. . . .

For a second she looks terribly wise and worldly, so funny, that look on Sara's face, like a white owl, her hair sticking up and around her head in a feather crown.

What difference would that make, dear? she says. Smirks. Positively.

Oh my, Sara. What a peek I got into *you,* just then.

Who did you love, Sara? Was it old Trevor all the way?

For a minute there. . . .

* * *

Once I told Ellie about an odd notion that popped into my head one day while sitting on Sara's couch and staring out the picture window at the brown, dirty yard.

Maybe I'm like God to Sara, I said.

God, Ellie said. That word makes me uneasy.

I know, I said. But I have to use it if I'm going to tell you about my idea.

And there is a sense in which you are God to me in the same way.

Then Ellie *really* looked uncomfortable. But I forged on. Never give up. Never give up.

Nothing is stirring. . . .

It's so quiet. . . .

Listen, Ellie, this is my thought: maybe the way I talk to Sara is the way God talks to me. I mean, maybe I'm asking the same dumb questions over and over, and He's giving me the answers, over and over, and I'm forgetting and asking again; you know the questions: Why is this happening?—what is the meaning of it all?—where am I going?—where have I been?—who am I?—like that. . . .

Over and over. Maybe I'm driving God crazy. I mean, maybe He has to exercise extreme patience and forbearance to keep from leaving me, like I don't leave Sara, won't, never will, Ellie, can't. . . .

Forbearance? said Ellie.

You know what I mean, I said.

Anyway, maybe God is to me as I am to Sara.

And maybe God even lies to me now and then. For my good. Couldn't this be?

I say.

Hm, she says. And: maybe Anthony would understand this. Maybe he could say something pertinent. I can't.

The whole concept disturbs me. She says.

I know, I say. But you being disturbed doesn't change it for me.

Anthony loved you, she says. Anthony loved you almost as much as he loved me. Maybe *as* much. . . .

Well, she says. But that's crazy to say. I was his *wife,* for heaven's sake. . . .

* * *

When I was living with Elinor and Anthony on Morton Street, one day I got a letter from Bud, saying that he thought we should consider ourselves engaged.

Engaged! I thought. Sure. Why not.

So I wrote back and said: Okay. We're engaged.

Ellie said when she heard: Isn't he going to give you a ring?

He doesn't believe in rings, I said.

He thinks they're, you know, terribly, well, conventional, and all. . . .

We think that.

Ellie looked horrified. And dubious. But don't you want a *ring?* she said.

I mean, Anthony is as *outré* as anybody, but he gave me a *ring.* . . .

Bud says a ring is a symbol of bondage, I said. I can see his point . . . and, I mean, what does it matter, a little piece of metal, a little piece of glass. . . .

My little girl, Ellie said. Engaged . . . god. . . .

She bought me a bracelet, made in Siam, Thailand now, silver and black, black somehow imposed on the silver and then carved through, so that deep silver designs gleamed against the black: a lovely, delicate thing.

You have to have *something* to commemorate an engagement, she said.

Anything as important as an engagement. . . .

And: *My little girl.* . . .

Honest to god.

I am *not* a little girl, I said: *Ellie!*

You are, she said.

You're only eight years older than I am: I said.

I'm a thousand years older than you are, she said.

* * *

When our first child, Bud's and mine, a boy, was born and died only a day later, we were in Minneapolis, at my parents' house, away from our home and our own things. I wanted to give my little baby, my little son, something to take with him, a present from his mother: like a toy, a toy to play with in heaven. . . .

All I had with me that had any value or meaning was that bracelet. So I gave it to Bud to give to my baby. There was a funeral, but I couldn't go, I was too sick—I gave the bracelet to Bud and asked him to put it into my child's hand and wrap it around his wrist so that he wouldn't lose it.

Now, whenever I remember that child, my little boy—and I remember him every day, seldom I think does a day go by that I do not flash on an image of him and flash away—I am, as I told you, sixty years old now, so it has been a long time—but I still remember, and when I remember, in that flash of memory I always see his body gone to bone, the bones of his tiny hand still clutching the bracelet from his Mama, the beautiful Siamese bracelet still wrapped around the bones of wrist.

Isn't that kind of morbid? says Ellie, when I tell her about this.
Yes, maybe, I say.
But done is done.
I say.
And can't be undone.

* * *

When Anthony was in the Vets' hospital in Augusta, I think it was Augusta, or maybe Savannah, so long ago now, that time after he tried to kill himself and didn't quite manage it and was so sick afterward—anyway, we went to see him in the hospital, Ellie and I.

We brought—strictly forbidden—big chunks of old-fashioned sweet chocolate for him because he said he was absolutely dying for chocolate. It was forbidden because his skin problem was just awful at the time, but we did it anyway.

Or tried to do it. God intervened, or something.

I packed the chocolate into my big straw purse and carted it past the nursing station and into the psych ward.

Don't act like it's so heavy, Ellie hissed in my ear. You're carrying it like it's heavy. . . .

They're going to be suspicious. . . .

Ellie, it *is* heavy, I said. I'm trying. This is not as easy as you think. . . .

We got the purse past the nurses and into the ward and down the aisle, past all the beds full of other vets, and we got it to Anthony's bed and then the bottom ripped out of the purse and all the chocolate fell out, crash, bash, clunk, all of it, and we stared at the disaster, and then we cracked up, all three of us, me, Ellie, Anthony, ha-ha-ha, ho-ho-ho, huh-huh, so funny, chocolate all over everything, all over the bed, all over the floor, wonderful chunks of sweet chocolate, so hard to find any more. . . .

We laughed too hard to think to rescue even one piece, and

Anthony laughed the hardest of all, huh, huh, that terrible liquid laughter; and the nurses confiscated all the chocolate, of course they did.

Just one piece, Anthony pleaded with them. Oh, please. Still laughing. How could they resist him?

But they did.

They took it all.

You know you can't have this, they said.

You know it's forbidden.

Don't you want to get well?

And we cracked up again.

No, he didn't want to get well. Of course he didn't.

* * *

When Anthony was so sick, at the end, and going to die before long, we all knew it, he asked me to write to him.

I do write to you, Anthony, I said. Every time I write to Ellie there is a message for you. In fact, everything I write to Ellie is just as much for you, for both of you . . . equally. . . .

By myself, he said.

Separately.

I want to be written to *separately*.

Cranky. He was so cranky. People who are dying I guess get cranky.

So I said I would, of course I did, we were all at that time giving Anthony anything he wanted because we were always so aware of the death in him, of the heart that was not going to beat much longer.

So: Okay, I said.

But it wasn't that easy.

I found that I had nothing to say to Anthony by himself.

Even the effort to do it made me feel terribly shy.

But I did write once, so that I did not absolutely break my promise to him. I found a card that said: *Things are getting worse, please send chocolate.* And I wrote one paragraph inside the card: nothing much, just *Dear Anthony, here is a card just for you, like I promised, blah, blah, blah.*

Well. You know the kind of thing. The weather's been awful. Margaret is fine. Blah, blah.

It couldn't have been very satisfying to him. It couldn't have been what he wanted from me. Lord knows what he wanted from me.

* * *

When he died, I came down to Atlanta and Elinor and I buried Anthony's ashes in a hole we dug among the roots of a pretty little dogwood tree in the backyard of the house on Beech Valley Road. We set a statue of Pan, maybe eighteen or twenty inches tall, to guard the grave, make sure that no wanton, restless spirit walked.

We found the Pan that morning in a courtyard display of plaster and concrete and marble memorials and garden pieces. I think we looked at hundreds of possibles: pudgy little boys, fountains, nymphs, what-have-you. No angels, we did not even consider angels.

Here's Pan, I said. And there he was, tucked into a dusty corner, the little goat-god, tootling his wanton pipe, laughing, leering just a bit, sneering, maybe. That's it, said Elinor. That's perfect.

Do you want to look at any more, I said. To be absolutely sure.

No, it's Pan, said Ellie. Pan is just right. Pan is perfect.

I agree, I said. It's Pan.

So we dug the hole and poured ashes into it from a plastic bag that was in a shoebox, no fancy urns for this crowd, and I stuffed the empty bag into the hole too because some ashes still clung inside the bag and I figured that all of Anthony had better go in. And then we covered the hole with the same earth we'd dug out of it and set the Pan there to watch. And finally we drank a little champagne and poured some into the earth of Anthony's grave.

It should have been chocolate, I said.

Yeah, but you can't do chocolate at a funeral, said Ellie. It isn't fitting.

Oh, I said.

* * *

Anyway, that's that. That's pretty much all of it—or as much as I need to tell for right now, as much as I *can* tell.

There are parts of every story that are better not told: parts you need to lie about, even.

God knows.

And maybe lies.

Sara and Anthony sit there in my memory together, hand in hand sometimes, on the blue couch, looking out the picture window at the brown garden, which will be a little Eden in a few months.

I am the connection.

Is it enough?

It has to be enough, it's all there is, there isn't any more . . .

Nothing is stirring . . .

The wooden bear sits on Anthony's piano in the house on Beech Valley Road. Sometimes someone picks the bear up, swirls the wooden ball; and the bear plays the little piano. One note, over and over, plunk, plunk.

From time to time, maybe once or twice a year, Ellie asks someone to come in to play on the big piano, so that the big piano does not die.

* * *

Once I introduced my father—who said I was on my way to Sodom, remember?—to a Lutheran minister of my acquaintance. The minister—not having, I guess, as I do not, a lot of small-talk—said, right off the bat: Do you believe in God, sir? And my father said: I believe in the invisible connection.

* * *

The agency has decided to pay extra for the four hours I come in before nine p.m. on Fridays. From five to nine. An overnight is nine p.m. to nine a.m., so you see, they *do* owe me.

It comes to a hundred dollars a month extra. Maybe even a little more. More like a hundred and ten.

So I only have to figure out where to get another ninety dollars a month.

It'll work out. You'll see. Everything always works out. One way or another, in this world or another, and in spite of appearances to the contrary, God saves us all.

We are all in terrible danger, but we must try anyway to be good. To behave.